A HOME ICE ROMANCE

SCORING Lacey

JENNA HOWARD

ISBN: 978-1-7751134-4-7

The last thing newly divorced Lacey Magerin wants is a relationship with Shayne Donnelly. The NHL goalie is ten years younger, her brother's best friend and he has no desire to be in Granville, Saskatchewan.

All she's trying to do is adapt to this new life where her husband left her for a twenty-two year old while her youngest daughter, a hurt, angry fifteen year old, blames her for the divorce. The last thing she wants or needs is a summer fling as her life unravels.

His hometown holds few good memories for Shayne. The Magerin family and hockey were all that kept him sane until hockey provided him with the permanent escape he needed from his drunk, abusive father. He's returned just long enough to participate in the yearly hockey game at the Magerin Hockey School and then he's out.

He has zero desire to remain in town so how is it that he's still sticking around? Two words: Lacey Magerin.

The rules in this new game are unclear but will that stop them from finding love in the least likely place – on home ice?

For the one person who gets really excited for me when I tell her I sold, and who doesn't mind when I tell her she's not allowed to read what I write because the first one shocked the heck out of her.

This one's for you, Mom (that grain elevator you'll never know about was just for you.)

Chapter 1

SHAYNE DONNELLY WONDERED what she was wearing under that little green dress. It was the neckline, he decided, that made him wonder. He was sure there was a technical term for the sequin fabric curving over her breasts like a lover's hands. He didn't care if they called it a dead-man-walking neckline. His finger itched to hook into the little dip between her tits and pull the glittery fabric down. Which nipple would he lick first? Left? Or right? It seemed very important for him to decide.

It was a dress meant for fucking. So was the woman.

The non-existent back curved over her plump ass…an ass that beckoned him to push that fabric up to her waist then bend her over the poker table. He'd fill his hands with that butt, parting the cheeks and then he'd bury his dick in her. He swore he felt that tight little hole stretching over his cock, felt her ass rubbing him as he plunged hard and fast.

He lifted his glass up as he next contemplated the

short length of dress she wore. It ended high above her knees, revealing the longest legs he'd ever seen. They'd wrap around him a few dozen times as he plopped her ass down on the dessert table and fucked her hard. Maybe he'd pop one breast into the chocolate fountain and lick her clean. He'd leave her killer heels on so he felt the sharp heels digging into his ass each time they slammed together.

God almighty, he wanted to fuck her.

He wanted to fuck Lacey Magerin--until last year, Lacey Magerin-Hodges.

His cock pounded with the need to claim her. Any way, every way. Over and over until they were both dead.

His thoughts were going to get him killed.

He sipped his scotch as he envisioned the woman writhing naked in his thoughts. This was Lacey, he told himself. Lacey. Not some puck bunny who screwed around with anyone who had a helmet. She was a mother for crying out loud. The mother of teenage daughters at that. She was the oldest sister of his best friend. She had driven him and her brother Todd to hockey practice when they were kids. Damn it, she had even babysat him a couple of times. She had taught him and Todd how to drink when they turned nineteen.

None of this was helping drive the prurient thoughts from his brain. It was that green dress. He knew it. He never would have looked at her if she had been wearing black.

Maybe.

Maybe he needed to get laid.

A few of the ladies at the fundraiser were puck bunnies. He could tell. Sure they wore fancy dresses but they still wanted to sleep with hockey players. Any hockey player would do. Their panties dropped fast when the word NHL was tossed about. They didn't care about him as a person, only that he was a goalie for the Houston Steam. His gaze scanned the room before returning to Lacey.

"Who's the babe?"

Shit. He took another sip, contemplating the level of alcohol in his glass. Too much to excuse himself to the bar. Adam Payne stood beside him, drinking imported beer. The man crapped gold out of his ass and played centre like an assassin--fast and lethal, especially with his slap shot. They didn't get along. Never had, never would. Payne thought the world owed him because he could play hockey and was the son of a former mayor.

The two of them competed hard throughout their time at Magerin Hockey School. Shayne determined to prove to himself he wasn't like his drunk of a father and Payne determined to remind Shayne he didn't belong at the expensive school. They didn't play the same position, nor on the same NHL team. That didn't mean they didn't try to flatten the other when they were on the same ice.

The press fed off the rivalry.

"Hm?" Shayne watched as Payne's ice blue eyes immediately sought out Lacey. Her back was to them and Shayne wanted to pour his drink along that smooth plane of skin, then sip the expensive scotch from her skin. Paradise.

Payne just smirked and sipped his beer. Shayne fought the urge to punch him in the face. "Less watching from the bench, Donnelly." He slapped Shayne on the back and sauntered across the room to hit on Lacey. Shayne decided not to warn him the woman was Lacey. This would be entertaining.

Fuck--unless she decided to sleep with Payne.

No, she wouldn't do that. She was smart. Sex with Adam Payne would be...unbelievably stupid. That's what Shayne told himself anyway.

He watched the approach of the NHL bad boy. As a waiter passed, Payne plucked a glass of champagne off the tray. He spoke to her back. The face-off would undoubtedly be something sexy. She turned. Home team grabs the puck. Visitors scramble. Grinning now, Shayne wandered over to the bar and ordered two Glenfiddich. Whistling the "Hockey Night in Canada" theme song, he approached the pair where home ice still had the advantage.

He had to give Payne credit. He tried to make it look like he hadn't been hitting on her. He really did.

"You look stunning, Lace." Shayne handed over the second drink and earned a smile.

"Thanks Shayne, you read my mind."

"That you're stunning?" Shayne met her gaze. In those towering heels they were the same height. "It's a gift."

An unladylike snort came from her as she took a sip. "I needed this."

"When one gets hit on by Payne, alcohol is usually required."

She grinned suddenly, her eyes crinkling around the corners while her nose made a little wrinkle. Payne called him a cocksucker under his breath while Lacey smacked his arm lightly. "You are so bad. You clean up pretty good though. A tux." She bobbed her eyebrows up and down as she adjusted the shoulder of his jacket.

"What do you know?" Payne took a sip of his beer and gave Shayne a bored look. "You can clean up a dirt farm boy."

Lacey's eyes narrowed as she plucked a non-existent piece of fluff off Shayne's jacket. Shayne took a sip of his drink, ignoring Payne. He had been called worse by better men.

"I like a little dirt under the nails," Lacey said as she gave Payne a slow look up and down. "It gives a man character. Excuse us. Shayne promised me a dance."

He couldn't help his smirk as he took another sip of his drink then set the glass down on a table. "Can't let a lady down. See you on the ice, Payne."

"Count on it," the other man growled.

Every July when school was out, the annual fundraiser for the Magerin Hockey School also included a hockey game. A little over thirty-three years ago, Lacey's father, Coach Magerin, had retired from his short stint in the NHL. Coach had told Shayne it was because his family was growing, his home was here. Somehow Coach had gotten the idea to start up a hockey school. From kindergarten to grade twelve, students enrolled where they got regular schooling and learned hockey. There had been classes on contracts in high school, public relations and even how to find an agent. The Magerin Hockey School was why Granville had turned into a successful city in Saskatchewan. The news called their growing city the hockey capital of Canada. Some major companies had even relocated their headquarters here so kids could go to school because the odds were high that a kid who attended MHS would make it into the big league. Tonight's fundraiser was for the scholarship program. Shayne had been a scholarship kid, so even when he didn't attend he sent in a healthy chip. Without MHS, Shayne would never have escaped Granville.

Considering a lot of the alumni had gone on to play in the NHL or on the Canadian national team, the annual alumni game was always a good one.

Lacey set down her own drink along with a little gold purse that matched her heels. They walked towards the dance floor where couples were currently swaying to a Frank Sinatra song. The music ranged all over the place. Earlier he had watched Lacey's mother, Dana Magerin, rocking out to AC/DC.

"Thirty years old and he's still an asshole," Lacey said as stepped into his arms.

Wow. She smelled really, really good. Dancing with her was not a brilliant idea.

"At ninety-five he'll still be an asshole." There was nowhere to put his hand but on her back. Her soft, silky back. I am not getting a hard-on dancing with Lacey. I am not getting a hard-on dancing with Lacey.

He fought the urge to spread his fingers on all that warm skin and pull her close so her body rubbed against his hard-on. Her dark hair was pulled up into some kind of girly twist with curls tumbling down around her face, to the base of her neck. He wanted one of those curls to coil around his cock as she went down on him. Fuck. Donnelly, get a grip on reality and not your dick.

"I'm trying to remember the last time you were here for one of these things." Whiskey bronze eyes searched his face, a little frown between her elegant eyebrows.

Really? Elegant eyebrows? He was a sick, sick man. "Four years ago." Four years ago she had been married. The asshat had up and run off with a twenty-two year old last year. "How you holding up? Want me to beat your ex-husband with my stick?"

"Absolutely, but can we discuss the beating later? I want to enjoy myself tonight." Her smile looked strained around the edges. Oh yeah, he was so going to beat up the asshat.

"Then you shall. Ready?" Before she could ask ready for what, he took her spinning across the dance floor in a series of quick turns. He brought her to a controlled stop, continuing to dance while she laughed with delight. Much better than her earlier attempt.

"Well, well, don't you have hidden talents. Do it again."

He did, managing to navigate them around the other dancers. At least it was a distraction from the arousal nipping at his system. Crap. He wished he had never noticed her. Could he go back to the moment when she was only his best friend's older sister?

"You seem to know exactly what I need tonight." She met his gaze, a soft smile appearing. "Thanks, Shayne."

"More booze?" His naked body covering her naked body?

"God, yes."

Reluctantly he released her and took her back to the tall table where their drinks waited. He rested his forearms on the table as he scanned the crowd. He spotted his friend, Todd Magerin, at the roulette wheel. His gaze shifted back to the woman. She was gorgeous.

Long, wavy chestnut hair, eyes the colour of whiskey in a dark room, the Magerin nose that was a little big at the tip and a succulent mouth he definitely imagined wrapped around his cock. Her skin was almost copper in colour and she had the most luscious ass.

She had modelled in her late teens and early twenties, even with a baby on her hip. Until the asshat had nipped that in the bud because he refused to have a successful wife. Irony was he had been her agent so he had to have known that those lean inches would make a successful model.

"You're staring."

Screw it. "You are one gorgeous woman."

She paused in sipping her drink, studying him. "This a sudden realization?"

He tilted his head. "Yeah."

A snort escaped her. "Thanks, babycakes."

Mayday! Mayday! Shayne caught her wrist when she went to walk away. "Before you were Todd's beautiful oldest sister. But now," he lifted a shoulder in a shrug even as the voice in his head told him to pull up before he crashed and burned, "you're a gorgeous woman."

Sweet God, would someone shut him up? He was not usually this idiotic around women. He was stumbling in the dark because all of a sudden Lacey was this tasty morsel he wanted in his mouth. Her gaze flicked over his face before she looked away.

"Uhm-hm," she responded, clearly flustered.

Smooth, Donnelly. So smooth. He swallowed the rest of his drink and searched for an escape route. He had mentally mocked Payne and now here he was, no better. Awesome.

"Did you want a play air hockey?"

"What?" His brain couldn't keep up as he gazed at the woman beside him.

"Air hockey. Couples tournament. Someone needs to kick my parents' asses this year. I think we can take them."

He stared at Lacey, his mind churning the words around. "Yeah," he said slowly as a grin emerged on his face. "I think we can take them."

"Keep it clean, Magerins," the ref said. Walter Lewis was one of her parents' best friends, the father of her own best friend and was this year's emcee and referee. He was dapper in his tuxedo, his gaze shifting between the two teams. Lacey expected him to say 'touch gloves' like they were in a boxing match.

"Yeah, yeah," Lacey said then snarled at her mother. Her mother's blue eyes narrowed in response. "You're going down, old lady."

"Watch your mouth," her mother snapped back and tightened her grip on the plastic mallet. She looked ferocious in her gold evening gown. The bodice hugged her mother's slender body and the starburst of gems added an extra sparkle. Her mom was gold from the tips of her heels to the elegant upsweep of her hair.

There were times Lacey felt her mom was too elegant for Granville, Saskatchewan. Until she opened her mouth and cursed like a trucker...or the wife of a hockey coach.

"Call it," said the referee.

"Heads," Shayne said beside her, glaring at her father. The two men had beady looks in their eyes, like gun shooters standing in the middle of town waiting for high noon.

Air hockey was taken very seriously with this crowd.

Walter flipped the coin. "Tails it is. Swap to the men at five points."

Favouritism. She knew it. She moved to her end of the table, not sure she wanted to be the red player. She wanted yellow. For no other reason than it would irritate her mother. "Take her down, sweetheart," her father said, his arms folded over his chest.

"We've got youth on our side, Coach," Shayne said. "You're what? Pushing ninety?"

Lacey fought a grin as her father glared. Seventy-one on his last birthday. Her mother pointed at Shayne. "You shut your yap, boy-o. I put Band-Aids on your skinned knees."

"Yes, ma'am."

"Asshole," her mother growled then the thin puck was dropped and Lacey went after it. Light streams of air brushed over her arm as she snapped the puck at the slot at her mother's end. In, damn it.

"Right on, sweetheart," her dad shouted as her mother blocked the shot. "Spank her."

Jesus. It had been awhile since she had played this. She hadn't participated in the games at the fundraiser in years because Kevin found them demoralizing. She blocked the shot and fired it back, her bracelet sliding back and forth on her wrist. Her mother blocked Lacey's shot, retaliating in kind. "Fuck," she muttered when the puck got past her and slammed into the slot. Her mother spun around and high-fived her dad then returned as Walter retrieved the puck.

"Hang on." Shayne leaned over the table. She stared at her wrist as his fingers brushed her skin. The same skittery feeling from when he had called her a gorgeous woman flittered in her stomach as he removed her bracelet and tucked it into his pocket. "Game on." He folded his arms over his chest. He looked intimidating, his hazel eyes flat in what she often referred to as his game face. Not even the tuxedo diminished that hard expression.

The man needed to wear a tuxedo more often. It hugged all that muscle perfectly. He was, she searched for the word, sexy.

She blinked twice as the puck sailed right by her. then looked up and over her shoulder, meeting Shayne's gaze.

"If you move your hand," he moved his side to side, "your chances of stopping shots increase."

"My team," she said, pointing at her chest. "You're on my team." Was it her or had his gaze flicked down to her cleavage before snapping back up to her face? What the hell was going on? What kind of drink had he given her? Shayne didn't look at her boobs, and she never used to notice he was sexy. He was Shayne for crying out loud. Her little brother's best friend.

Little. Brother.

Ten years younger than her. He wasn't sexy. He was

a kid.

He pointed down and she nodded, focusing on the game. The puck dropped, so to speak, and she went after it determined to not be beat by her sixty-eight year old mother. "Damn it," she snarled as her mother sank another goal.

This was embarrassing.

"Who's your mommy, little girl? Me." Her mom was pretty good at the trash talk as she pointed her fingers at herself then flicked them at Lacey in a "come and get it" wave.

This was mortifying.

"Don't shoot head on," Shayne said in a low voice, standing at her back. "Hit it off the boards."

"What? Why?"

"Trust me. Aim for where her champagne glass is. And don't move when she shoots. She's always head on and you're all over the place. Hold it in front of the slot."

"You told me to move it," she said, glaring at him.

"Well you were just standing there. At least make it look like you're moving. Fake it."

Okay. He was the pro here. She fought the urge to nod and returned to the game. She focused on the game, not the man behind her. Damned if his method didn't work.

She barely moved her paddle then when she saw her chance; she aimed at her mom's drink. The puck hit the low wall then bounced off and went into the slot, the sweetest vision ever. "Yes!" She punched her fists in the air. "Take that, old woman! Yes." She jammed her fingers towards her mother.

"Nicely done. This time block the left half of the slot then aim straight down the middle."

She turned to look at her partner. Shocked. She was shocked. "You're a hustler!"

He cleared his throat, his eyes twinkling so they looked more green than hazel. "I'm a goalie. She's predictable. Centre left right. You're watching the puck. I'm watching your mom."

"Awesome. We're kicking ass," she said with relish.

"We're down by two, doll. Don't get cocky."

She nodded the returned to the game and did what he said. Exactly. Scoring twice on her mom. "Oh yeah, who owns it. Huh? Huh?" She watched as her mom faced her dad for a meeting.

"He's about to tell her I cracked her pattern," Shayne said as he gave the couple a hard look.

"What? I did not!" Her mom yelled then spun around to give Shayne the evil eye.

"Would I do that to you?" He flattened his hand on his heart. "You're the beat in my pulse, Mrs. Magerin. The blood in my heart. Lacey is just that good."

Her dad glared. "Lay off, boy-o. Get your own woman."

"What do I do? Stop flirting with my mom and tell me what to do." Lacey swatted his chest and waited for her instructions. He glanced down at her and she found her thoughts wavering from the air hockey game. Had his mouth always been that sensual?

What the hell was going on?

She got the fact that it had been a long time since she had sex but that didn't mean she went around eyeing up her kid brother's friends. For crying out loud! Snap out of it.

"Repeat the pattern," he said as he took a fresh drink a waiter brought over.

"Are you drunk? What?" He had to be. Did he miss that part where he told her that the enemy now knew they had cracked her game?

He handed the glass to her, put his hands on her hips and turned her around. Her heart gave an idiotic extra thump as she sipped his drink. "Repeat the pattern," he repeated. His hands squeezed her and she almost dropped his glass. "Trust me."

What the hell was going on? She surrendered the glass, wiped her damp hands on her dress and faced her mom. Her heart was racing. She felt hot and itchy. She was too busy thinking of her malfunctioning body and her mother used that to her advantage. Damn it.

Focus on the game. She stared at the hand braced on the table not far from her. An athlete's hand, it was large like the rest of him with a broad palm. A finger pointed and she followed the direction to the game. The game, the game.

Right. Okay. Where were they?

"Left," he said softly.

"Right."

"No. Left."

She rolled her eyes but once more guarded the left then fired the shot. Slick as the scotch he was drinking, she made her shot, tying them up again.

She could do this then it would be up to him to win this. It wasn't an easy shot this time. The plastic puck made sharp sounds as it was pushed back and forth.

"Champagne glass," Shayne said into his glass.

She banked the shot and watched in total surprise as her puck went in. "Holy cow," she said quietly. "Holy cow!"

"Point to the red team. Five-four. Partner swap."

"Did you see that? Yes! Take that!" She gave a hip wiggle as she stuck her tongue out at her mother.

"Nothing like winning like an adult," her mother said with a dignified sniff, as if she hadn't started the trash talk. "Game's not over yet."

"Please. I have the best goalie in the NHL on my team. Who do you have? Retired left wing? Please," she snorted, waving her hand in dismissal. She glanced at the best goalie in the NHL and watched as he shrugged off his tuxedo jacket.

Holy.

Hell.

The white silk shirt hugged one broad chest. She wanted to stroke her hands over the breadth of his shoulders and down the soft fabric of his shirt to his ass. Shayne Donnelly had a fantastic ass. He folded the coat and handed it to her before he removed the green cufflinks from the wrists. He tucked them into his pants pocket and rolled up his sleeves.

Holy.

Hell.

Had his forearms always looked like that? They were tanned and roped with muscles. There was a tattoo around his left wrist. Had that always been there? She reached for his hand and turned it so she could see the design. It was the Granville Husks logo. On the inside of his arm were the two hockey stick blades that wrapped around his wrist, turning into wheat ears. Two zeroes were in green between the tip of the wheat and the stick blades. The year he had graduated from MHS. Crap, as if that wasn't reality right there.

He had left high school ten years ago. Ten!

"Have you always had this?"

"Five years." He took a sip of his drink and handed the glass to her, which meant he had it last time he was here but she hadn't noticed. "You ready, old man?"

"Bring it, kid." Her father had removed his jacket also. "You think you can take me? I know all your moves. I know for one you can't shoot for shit. That's why they put you in net."

"How're the joints? Arthritis acting up?" Shayne took the red paddle, spun it on the smooth surface of the table then settled into place. He crouched down like he was in the net, his legs spread and bent at the knees. He didn't look at anyone but her father, two warriors facing off.

Lights glinted off her dad's steel grey hair and his brown eyes were locked on Shayne as if the power to win was in his gaze alone. Her dad was competitive. His rule with hockey was to have fun but "Who says you can't have fun and win?" was often heard coming from his mouth more often than not. His nose had been broken a few times in the game and decades ago the top three teeth had been removed by a facer from a puck. His knee was shot, arthritis had kicked in, and none of it kept him off the ice – even now.

She loved every bump and line in his craggy face, but

he needed to go down.

The puck dropped and it was a vicious battle. She and her mother were amateurs in comparison to her father and Shayne. The puck was barely visible as it flew back and forth. She moved so she could watch them better. Shayne's gaze was everywhere as he tracked the puck with ease. Unfair.

Granted he was used to keeping his eye on the puck but, really, this was rubbing it in. His arm snapped forward and the puck was a blur as it flew over the little streams of air. Right past her father's yellow paddle and into the slot.

His eyebrows rose and fell. It was all the trash talk he did.

He settled back into position and this time she watched him instead of the game. He was utterly absorbed in the game, his gaze tracking and following, his hand barely seeming to move as he stopped shot after shot. No, he wasn't following the puck. He was anticipating. He was almost two seconds ahead of where the puck would go.

She watched as he delivered another hard shot, sinking it. Her father cursed and once more those eyebrows rose and fell. She sipped Shayne's scotch, enjoying the smoky flavour on her tongue as Shayne spun the paddle once more, letting the puck coast away before he recaptured it and hunkered down.

"This is almost sad," her brother said behind her. "Watching the old man get spanked like this."

She glanced at Todd who was smirking. "You bet on this game."

"Please. Shayne versus Dad? Everyone has bet on this game. It's like making a six-year-old go against the NHL. But Dad's needed to be knocked off this pedestal for a while. Way to kick Mom's ass."

"She's predictable."

He snorted as he squeezed her shoulder. Clearly he knew who had shared that wisdom. She looked at the game then back at her brother. He looked grown-up. When had that happened?

Like the other men in the room, he wore a tuxedo but with a green and yellow vest instead of a cummerbund. The colours matched the team colours for the Granville Husks. Usually his hair was a mess, the curls dominating but tonight it was almost smooth to his skull. He had tried shaving his head once. He did not have the right face and head shape to go without hair, even a crew cut. So it grew wild. Like him. Even his blue eyes looked older tonight. When had these two grown up on her?

Damn.

The third face off and once more the puck was being abused. She focused on the game. "He knows where Dad's aiming before Dad does. How does he do that?"

"He's good, Lace. He's really good. He can't shoot for shit though."

The puck hit the corner of the slot before her father knocked it away. Yeah, she thought, her brother was right. Every time Shayne missed a decent shot, his left eye twitched as if he was cursing in his head. On the outside though he was utterly calm.

Another point and his eyebrows bobbed.

Both Shayne and her father shook out their wrists.

The paddle made another slow, floaty spin as he stretched his arms over his head. The shirt strained over his chest and she wondered if every feminine heart fluttered in appreciation or if it was only hers.

"Feel the burn. You're going to choke," her father taunted.

"Only on the trophy, old man."

They had two more goals to go. Once more he was crouched down and the game was on. On the other side of the table were her two younger sisters cheering for their parents and taunting Shayne. He ignored them. She supposed if one was sometimes booed by twenty thousand people, her sisters were white noise. Although if Shelley, the second of the five Magerin kids, had been in town, odds are he wouldn't have been able to ignore them. She was the loudest of all the Magerins, including their mom.

She watched his mouth move. Watched his lips form, "fuck" a second before the puck few past him.

"Haha!" Her father crowed while her sisters and mom cheered, lipping off at the goalie.

Shayne rested his hands on his hips, ignoring the trash talk, his gaze skating over the table as if he was replaying the game. He looked up, met her gaze then he grinned. He winked before he bent down, focusing on the game. "Like you can do that again," he said.

"Watch me, kid. Watch me then you can weep tears when I beat your ass."

"Bring it."

IT WAS A beautifully tacky trophy, shaped like an air hockey mallet with "2010 Champions" on a little plaque. Actually, she was pretty sure it *was* a mallet that had been spray-painted gold. "I think I'll put it on the fireplace mantle. That will burn their asses every time they come over to visit me."

"You? Why do you get to keep it?" Shayne sat across from her, legs stretched out as he closed his eyes. It was tempting to rest her feet on top of his. She resisted. His jacket lay tossed over a chair and he hadn't bothered to roll down his sleeves. His forearms were really, really distracting with their dark brown hairs and that tattoo.

"It was my idea," she said as she sipped her celebratory glass of champagne. "We crushed them."

"We?"

"Okay. Me." He chuckled as he opened one eye, looking at her. Quite a few people were outside, enjoying the warm weather. A fire snapped at the other end of the patio and a couple cuddled on the sofa before it. "Isn't it pretty? Prettier than that Stanley Cup you won. What a hunk of junk."

She couldn't count how many barbecues had been hosted out here before a Granville Husks hockey game. It was hard to believe they were at a hockey arena as tea lights flickered and glowed from where they hung in small glass lanterns. Clusters of comfortable chairs were intimate and had more candles flickering in tall glass cylinders, adding to that soft, glowy feeling.

"Yes. They should use the Cup for scrap. I didn't get to keep that one either." He sighed heavily. "So is the lot of a hockey player's life." He uncoiled from his slouch and grabbed her trophy.

"Hey, that's mine."

A dark eyebrow arched up. His lashes lifted and she found herself staring into eyes that were more gold than hazel at the moment from the flickering candles. That skittery feeling moved through her again.

She was a fairly confident woman but this was knocking for a loop. Whatever *this* was. He leaned forward and set the trophy in her hand. Without breaking her gaze, his fingers slid down to her wrist where her pulse was jumping erratically from his touch and the man. *It's Shayne,* she told her hormones. *Yum* they purred in response.

She was thankful her dress was heavy from the sequins because then he'd know her nipples were swelling from that light touch, from his eyes. Like with the game, he seemed to see everything at once. He tugged as she leaned forward, drawn by his golden eyes and sensual mouth.

He tasted of scotch.

It registered in her head as their open mouths met, tongues seeking the other. Her left brain snapped out words like Shayne, younger, brother's, best friend.

It was hard to listen when his tongue slid and thrust into her mouth. She curled her free hand around his neck as she changed the angle of her head for a better taste. He released her hand and cupped the back of her head as their mouths mated.

She couldn't remember the last time anyone had kissed her like this. It was tongues, it was heat, it was hunger. "This is crazy," she panted against his mouth, pulling an inch away.

"Yes," he said before he dragged her back, feasting on her mouth. A tug and she was draped over his lap. Beneath her ass she felt the hard evidence of his arousal as she met every hungry surge of his tongue with her own. "All night," he muttered into her mouth as she stilled on him, absorbing the feel of the firm flesh beneath fabric. "All night."

"God," she breathed before she drew him back down. Every glide of his tongue made her ache and throb. A large hand flattened on her thigh, slid down to her calf then back up. She gripped the back of his shirt as she pressed her breasts against him.

His hand slid up over the dress and curled into her ass. She gasped at the sensation. He squeezed her slowly, as if he was savouring the feel. They froze, lips touching as they both breathed heavily. She tried to tell herself she was sitting on the lap of a guy who hadn't seen thirty yet, that he was her brother's best friggin' friend.

Too bad the thoughts were obliterated by the hard press of his cock against her hip and the hand squeezing and releasing her ass. Her eyes opened and he was looking at her. "What?"

"I want to make you come," he said as his fingers traced the hem of her dress. "Right here. Right now."

Jesus. God. Almighty.

Her pussy spasmed at the words, at the look in his eyes. This was *not* the Shayne Donnelly she knew.

"Then I want to take you home." His hand slipped under her dress. His palm was hot on her ass. "Where I'll set you on the edge of your bed. I'm going to peel these tiny panties down then I'm going to make you come again. My mouth buried in your pussy."

Her heart thundered hard and fast as she stared at this stranger she had known his entire life. He rubbed her butt cheek. "Shayne," she whispered his name, incapable of any other sound.

"I bet you taste as good as I imagine. Then I'm going to flip you over, stand between your legs and bury my cock deep in you until you're screaming my name." He exhaled slowly as his hand moved to her hip. "Now's the time to say no."

No? Was he nuts? She grabbed the front of his shirt and pulled him down. She saw the flash of a smile before his mouth claimed hers as his fingers slid between her legs. He swallowed her cry of shock and she tasted his moan. She was wet. So wet.

Aching for him. Those clever fingers pushed aside the swatch of her thong and she arched into him as he found her clit. The orgasm hit her fast and hard. His mouth muffled her cries as she came immediately.

"Stop stop stop," she pleaded as her body spiralled out of control. She was shaking from the climax and the man. Against her she felt the soft fabric his pants, his hard cock and his fingers still lightly stroking her.

She stared at him, stunned.

"Been a while?"

She nodded and her lashes lowered. A while? She was pretty sure she hadn't come like that in years. "Shayne."

"Lacey."

"Take me home." He grinned before his mouth claimed hers. She moaned as he pushed a finger into her. "Holy God!" Her body arched hard as he began to move in her, slow thrusts as if he had all the time in the world. His thumb stroked through the growing wetness until he reached her clit and she nearly catapulted off his lap. She leaned against his other arm, his fingers caressing the swell of her breast bared by her strapless dress. His tongue plunged and stroked hers as he slid a second finger into her surging body. "Oh God, Shayne."

"Come for me, Lace."

She bit her lip and his mouth muffled her cry when his other hand slipped under her dress and pinched her nipple. The orgasm crested less violently than her first one. His fingers pushed relentlessly in her, picking her up and throwing her into the heated pleasure. She arched up into all that hard muscle as she climaxed again. She felt cream spill from her, over his fingers and onto his slacks. She flattened her hand over his cheek as they kissed through the quivers of her body. His fingers retreated and she felt him ease her thong back into place, along with her dress.

"Taste." Damp fingers rubbed her lips then vanished into his mouth.

Her tongue darted out to taste herself. He adjusted her top and bottom then leaned down to pick up a shoe that had fallen off.

She was having a heart attack. He eased the heel on then caressed up her leg again. "This is beyond crazy."

"Yes." He kissed her then lifted her off his lap.

Her thighs were quivering as she stood before him. Quivering! She gazed down at him and wondered if she was going to do this. She felt the stickiness between her thighs from her orgasms.

He reached over, grabbed his jacket and her trophy then stood up. When had she let it go? He eased the jacket on and she found herself glancing down. Her eyes widened to see the thick bulge tenting the slacks. "Oh dear."

"Want to kiss it and make it feel better?"

"Yes," she answered without a thought. She reached down to brush the back of her fingers over him. He caught her wrist with his lightning fast reflexes. She pouted. He turned her hand then pushed his hips forward so he filled her palm.

"Promise?"

She stared into his gaze and squeezed him. "Yes."

His lashes flickered as he exhaled. "Nice. Where's your purse?"

She looked around for it and saw his jacket had been covering it up. His hand flattened on the small of her back and she shivered at the contact. They walked around the outside of the most important building at MHS, the rink that had been converted for tonight's party.

Was she really going to do this? Have sex with her baby brother's best friend?

She glanced at him as he navigated them to her car. Growing up she had vowed never to have a station wagon. And there it sat in all its red shiny glory, her Subaru Outback. Her mother had smirked in retro victory. At least hers was sexier than her mom's had been in the 70s. And it was red--with no faux wood paneling. Eat your heart out, Mom. Shayne plucked her purse from where it was tucked underneath her arm and found the keys. He opened the passenger door and she sat down.

Maybe she was drunk. It would explain everything.

She felt drunk. Hot and dizzy.

He shut the door and walked around. He moved with fluid grace, as if he was on skates. Resting her head on her seat, she watched as he sat beside her. He slid the key into the ignition then stared out the windshield. Had he changed his mind? Was reality intruding on his brain too?

He moved fast for a large man.

He twisted and leaned towards her, spearing his hand into her hair, destroying the updo she had spent a fortune on. His mouth covered hers in a hungry, hot kiss. Her arm hooked around his neck as she pressed into him. His other hand tugged her gravity defying dress down and she gasped to feel his hand cover her breast, fingers stroking her aching, swollen nipple.

His mouth slid away, down her neck and over the tip where his fingers played. She cried out to feel the heat of his mouth, the stroke of his tongue, the sting of his teeth. The strength of suction had her arching of the seat and into him. He captured her other breast with his large hand and she gripped his head.

"Shayne!"

"God, your tits, Lace." He licked the crest of one breast, sucking the flesh into his mouth while his fingers tugged on her nipple. "They're amazing."

"Are you kidding?"

He lifted his head and his eyes were glazed and golden. "I so want to fuck your tits, Lacey."

She blinked and looked down at her breasts that were approaching their fortieth birthday this summer. She looked at him. "You do?"

"Oh yeah." He rubbed the heel of his hand over her nipple. "I really do."

She sighed, "Okay." She dragged his mouth back to hers. No one had ever wanted to fuck her breasts. Ever. Kevin had lost interest in them years ago. He had lost interest in her altogether shortly after.

Sex with her ex had never been like this though. Hungry and wild and needy.

Shayne lifted his head and flatted a hand between her breasts, rubbing up and down. His eyes lost focus as if he was imagining it was his cock instead of his hand. "This is crazy," he said as he swept his hand over her breast. His touch was almost reverent as he caressed up to her shoulder then down her arm. His fingers shackled her wrist and he met her gaze as he guided her hand to his groin. His lashes lowered as she felt him thick under the fabric.

"Crazy," she repeated, her other hand flattened on his

chest. She knew she didn't push him, he was rock solid muscle but he moved, leaning against the driver's door so she could explore him. A harsh sound came from him, his fingers cinching hard, as she traced the shape of him. He was big, she thought, which made sense. He was six feet three inches and about two hundred pounds. He was big for a goalie and yet it didn't slow him down.

He groaned and she liked the way his mouth parted as he arched beneath her caressing.

"Do you want to fuck my mouth too?"

He looked at her, his face in shadows. "Baby, I want to fuck every inch of you."

She felt moisture spill from her pussy as she shifted so she could kiss him. "Now?"

"Fuck." His hands fisted in her hair. She felt a pin fall down her back as curls spilled down around her shoulders. He feasted on her mouth, a man starved for her. *For her.*

A few cars down an alarm beeped and headlights flashed.

"Fuck," he said again and eased her back. He battled his way out of his jacket and eased it over her shoulders. "Not the place, Magerin."

She smiled as his hand shook. The engine rumbled to life and he exhaled loudly. An arm rested on the steering wheel while he stared at her. She grabbed the front of his jacket and flashed him. His smile was slow and sexy. He put the car into reverse then they were leaving Magerin Hockey School for her house.

Reaching under the jacket she wiggled the dress down and off. The car veered left then jerked back into the right lane. "Something wrong?" She felt decadent as she tossed her dress into the backseat.

"Nope," he said slowly as his hand caressed up her leg. "This is where you tell me you don't have condoms. And that the girls are home." He eased the car to a stop and gazed at her.

The heat in his eyes made her stomach jump nervously. Was she really going to do this?

Jesus. Condoms. Why would she have condoms? She shook her head. "Kayla's still in Calgary and Carmen went to a sleepover."

"Perfect." His gaze skimmed over her. "Don't move. At all." He vanished and she watched him jog across the street to the twenty-four hour convenience store. Five minutes later he came back, carrying a plastic cup in his hand. He lifted it up, sipping while he waited for a car to pass by. He grinned mischievously as he climbed into the car. "Slurpee?"

She took the cup and sipped the sweetened ice drink. "Good."

"Hydration's important." He began to drive again. "And ice is fun." He reached over, pressed his finger over the mouth of the straw as he drove the familiar route to her house. He brushed aside the jacket then when the plastic scoop on the end of the straw rested on her breast, he lifted his finger and the frosty drink spilled over her breast. She gasped at the sensation, goosebumps pebbling on her skin. At a stop sign, he leaned over and licked her. "Lots of fun." He kissed her then turned left. "Wanna open up that garage so you're not flashing the neighbourhood."

"Hm?" She blinked then opened the glove compartment when he pointed at the garage door. She handed over the remote and sipped the drink, watching this man she no longer knew.

Once the engine was off and the door was down, they were cocooned in silence. She watched him as she nervously nibbled on the straw. He was leaning forward again, his arm resting on the steering wheel as he stared at her.

They could stop here, she realized. Chock it up to a lot of scotch and an adrenaline rush from the game. She reached out with a hand cold from the cup and rubbed her wet finger over his mouth. He was beautiful.

Dark hair, eyes almost grey in the shadows, stubborn jaw. There was a scar under his chin from a hockey stick meeting his face. She traced the mark and met his gaze. "Take me upstairs, Shayne. Strip off my panties and make me come by your mouth. Then flip me over and fuck me until I come screaming your name."

He smiled as he caught her hand and kissed her palm. They both opened their doors at the same time and left the safety of the garage for the reality of her home.

She was going to do this. She was really going to do this.

When Kevin had left her, she had made over her bedroom. No more beige walls, no more asexual sheets. The furniture was new, the dark red bedding was new, the pale gold walls were new. He was, she realized, the first man in her new room. Nerves pricked at her as she folded her arms over her chest. He toed off his black dress shoes then walked towards her.

Lacey's heart galloped in her chest as he approached. He crouched down and brushed his fingers over her ankles. She gripped his shoulder as she shifted her balance. He gazed up at her as he palmed one stiletto off then set her foot down. Hands caressed slowly up her leg, moved to the other then stroked down. She lifted her left foot and the shoes were history.

He moved to his knees, his face level with her stomach as he idly ran his fingers up and down her legs.

"Why am I nervous?"

He slid his hands up under the jacket, caressed her ass then down to her ankles. Up and down, slow, measured strokes. "Because everything changes now. Now we're two people. A man wanting a woman, a woman wanting a man. The minute I slide into your body, I become your lover, not your kid brother's friend." His fingers curled and he drew her panties down, his fingers still managing to caress her. He had calluses from the game and they rasped over her skin with a sensual texture. She lifted one foot then the other. "It all changes now, Lacey," he said and lowered his mouth to her.

She cried out, dropping her hands to clutch his head as his tongue licked over her. He licked slowly, indulging himself. "Shayne." She gripped him as the tip of his tongue slipped between the damp folds and sought out her clit. "Shayne!" Her knees buckled and he moved her to the bed.

She sank onto her back as he spread her legs wide, opening her up and making room for those shoulders of his.

"Pretty pussy," he said before he lowered his head and pressed an open mouth kiss over her. She cried out, arching up as he proceeded to feast on her. He sucked, he licked, and he slid his tongue into her. She bowed, screaming when he bit her clit.

Holy God. What was he doing?

He bit her thigh, caressed her leg then returned to the promise he had made earlier. He dined on her pussy. Lips, tongue, teeth. They were everywhere. Her eyes snapped open she felt his tongue slowly circle lower. Never, ever, ever.

"When I said I was going to fuck you everywhere, Lace?" A finger replaced his tongue. "I meant it. Even here."

God, she thought as his mouth returned to her pussy, tongue boldly thrusting as his finger lightly brushed over the soft skin at her ass. "Shayne!" His fingertip eased in and she felt his mouth move as cream spilled from her. The minute stretching was as disconcerting as him putting his finger there. *Never, ever, ever,* she thought, *has anyone done this.* His hand caressed down her leg then he lifted her foot to his shoulder.

A soft kiss was pressed at the curve of her knee and then he lifted her leg over his head, rolling her onto her stomach. "This ass," he said with a little awe, his hands pushing up the jacket. "This luscious ass."

Lying on her stomach, she propped herself up on her elbows and gazed at the man staring at her ass like it was the most amazing thing he had seen. Kevin had called it her bubble butt, had made her work the Stairmaster in an attempt to deflate it. Hadn't worked. Her ass was her ass. "Luscious?"

"Plump and ripe." He met her gaze as he bit one cheek hard. She gasped, her back arching at the sensation. His eyes gleamed as he reached up and tugged on the back of his jacket. She sank down and let him strip it away. She rose once more, needing to see him.

"Fuck, Lace." He caressed up her legs, over her bum, up her back then down. When he stood up, he lifted her legs, scooting her forward to rest her knees on the bed. The joys of strength. "Sweet God," he whispered as his hand glided over her ass then down to her pussy.

She sank down, shuddering out a sigh as he caressed her with one hand. His other hand was coasting over her ass. His eyebrows rose and fell right before he delivered a loud, hard slap to a cheek. She cried out at the sensation, her hands fisting on the sheets. Holy hell, what was the man doing to her?

She felt herself spill over his fingers from the spank. He grabbed her and tossed her easily so she was on her back. She bounced twice before he was lying on her, his mouth claiming hers.

Her legs wrapped around his waist, pulling him close while her hands discovered how wide his shoulders were. "Naked, Shayne. Get naked. I want to see you." He rose up on his knees and she watched in delighted horror as he grabbed the front of his silk shirt and ripped it open. God, he was hard everywhere. Muscles carved his flesh, dark hair covered his chest before disappearing behind his cummerbund. She scrambled onto her knees, her hands exploring all that tanned skin. He struggled out of the ruined shirt that looked like it cost the same as one of Kayla's courses.

Had she ever been this hungry for a man?

Considering her sexual experience was the sum total of Kevin until tonight, the answer was an easy no.

She followed the pleated satin of the cummerbund to the back where she eased it open then tossed it aside. The front of his slacks tented over his erection. She gazed into Shayne's eyes as she opened the fly. His eyes narrowed to gold slits when she pushed the pants down over lean hips. Her fingertips barely brushed over him, before he grabbed her arms and flipped her onto the bed. He drew a small box out of the left pocket and tossed it beside her. His hand went into the other pocket and another small box landed on her bed.

"Did you buy in bulk?"

"The selection sucked." He stood up and stripped.

There should be a law for him to walk around naked. Her gaze couldn't settle anywhere. There was so much of him to take in. Shayne Donnelly was naked in her bedroom. Gloriously, beautifully naked. On her knees, she shuffled to the edge of the bed.

The backs of her fingers brushed over his stomach, the silky path of hair. Resting her head on his chest, she watched her hand lightly explore his abdomen. Fingers tunnelled into her hair and she felt him untangle the hairpins. His hand fisted in the silky strands and he pulled insistently, tilting her head up. His mouth took hers as her fingers stroked along the fullness of his cock. His mouth was hard on hers while her hand was light on him, a teasing caress. At the swollen plump head, he was wet. He continued to pull on her hair, dragging her down to the bed.

She gasped at the sensation, at the moisture weeping from him. Once more she was prone on the bed, looking up at him.

Had her ex stared at her like that? Like she was the sexiest creature he had ever seen? If he had, it was so long ago she had forgotten when.

Emboldened by the desire in his eyes, her fingers curled over the thickness of him. Caressing down to the base, she rejoiced in bringing forth the groan from him. A hand gripped her thigh and he drew her legs apart, opening her up.

Lacey was positive her heart was going to erupt out of her chest as he picked up one of the discarded boxes, withdrawing a condom. Her pussy contracted at the sight because it meant he was going to be inside her soon.

She watched as he sheathed himself in the thin latex, dislodging her hand. Fingers slid between hers and he leaned down, pinning her hand over her head.

"Hi," he said as he searched her gaze.

"Hi." Her foot caressed up his leg, curving over his ass. She pushed down while arching up. "Shayne, please." She wasn't sure she could tolerate much more of his foreplay. "I want you in me."

"Now?"

"Right. Now."

"Okay."

She would've grinned had he not chosen that moment to slide into her. She cried out, arching up at the sensation. Sex was an almost hazy memory as he stretched her with the slow, relentless entry.

"Fuck you're tight, Lacey." He flexed his hips forward. "Good?"

"Yes," she moaned as she wrapped her other leg around him. "Shayne." He eased out and she loved the feeling of him gliding in her. The returning stroke filled her. "Shayne." She gripped his hair with her free hand, tightening around his with her other. She lifted her head up. "Fuck me, Shayne."

His nostrils flared and he took her mouth while taking her at her word. He fucked her. Hard. Fast. He knew how to control his body, when to take her hard, when to slow it down, drawing it out.

She moaned his name, meeting the rhythmic thrusts. He shifted her, drawing her leg up to his shoulder. He caressed her ass. "Want to feel this ass." He eased out, rolled her onto her stomach then dragged her down the bed, sheathing himself in her once more. She cried out at the sensation, grabbing the red and white quilt. He rode her hard, driving into her as he fisted her hair in his hand once more, twisted her head so the bed wasn't muffling her cries.

"Shayne. Shayne!"

"Come, Lacey." He grabbed one of her hands, gripping hard. "Come, goddammit."

She felt every stroke in her pussy, against her ass. "Coming, Shayne."

"Yes, you are," he said as he eased his hand under her. One brush over her clit and she erupted. He fucked fast and pressed his face against her neck as she felt the hard jerks, felt him bite her, felt him shudder as he came. Another twist of her head and he kissed her as he sank onto her, a heavy weight she loved.

He untangled from her, tossed the condom into the trash can then pulled her up the bed. She felt boneless as he sank down beside her, dragging the quilt over her. She snuggled against him and inhaled the faint sandalwood cologne clinging to his sweat dampened skin.

She'd worry about the consequences later. Right now she wanted to luxuriate in this man in her bed. Tomorrow could wait. Resting her head on the solid curve of his pec, she listened to his heart thump as he caressed her back.

There was a sigh before he tumbled her onto her back and kissed her in another one of those devouring kisses that was all tongue and hunger. He braced himself above her and she caressed the muscles on his back. He was sinewy and bulky in the right places. "Are you staying?"

He searched her face. "I told you I was going to fuck every inch of you, Lacey. I haven't, yet."

She traced his mouth. It was masculine and sensual. Her fingernail scraped the shallow bow of his upper lip. What was he doing here with her?

Hell, what was she doing here with him?

"Good," she said as she caressed his leg with her foot. She liked the tickle of the hairs.

"Good," he repeated as he kissed her slowly. He shifted her onto her side. "Now sleep. I need the energy for the rest of your sixty-nine inches. One down, sixty-eight to go."

His arm banded over her stomach.

Her emotions were in turmoil on him being in her

bed. The breathing against her hair slowed, deepened.

She had sex with her brother's best friend. She had babysat him a few times. He was ten years older than Kayla, ten years younger than Lacey. Ten! Jesus.

"Stop thinking, I'm trying to sleep," he mumbled against her ear, his arm giving a little squeeze. "Sixty-eight to go. Need rest."

"What are we doing, Shayne?"

"Not sleeping?" He rolled her onto her back and loomed over her. "I apparently didn't do my job right because your brain still works." He grabbed the quilt and with a flick of his wrist, tossed it to the food of the bed. "Let me know when it stops." He rose up and crawled down her, wedging his way between her legs.

"Shayne!" She bowed up when his tongue swirled around her clit, the tip teasing her until she shifted under him. He settled her legs over his shoulders without breaking the circling. He squeezed her hips, caressed down to her ass and tilted her up when he sucked hard on her now aching clit. "God!" She grabbed the pillow under her with one hand and his head with the other.

A finger pushed into her, copying the circles he was once more making with his tongue. When he began to suck again, his finger thrust within her and she writhed under him.

Not even her husband had gotten this intimate with her body. He looked at oral sex the way he had looked at her – bothersome and inconsequential.

"Still thinking? Yeah, still thinking," he returned to her pussy.

When his finger eased out of her, she moaned a *no*

only to have his mouth replace it. Against her ass she felt that damp finger press, slowly, slowly, slowly.

"Shayne!" Her eyes snapped open and she arched hard when she felt his finger slid into her ass. A wicked chuckle was muffled against her before tongue and finger began to fuck her. The dual sensation snapped her brain apart. She felt it go seconds before he brought her to climax.

"Gotta see this." His hand slid under her and he lifted her up, his finger continuing the slow plunges in and out. "Oh, baby doll, this ass is begging for my cock. Still thinking, I see." He lowered her and returned to his feast until another orgasm shattered her into a million gooey pieces. He eased his finger from her, then returned to his original position.

She stared up at him with his mouth damp from her orgasms. She hooked her arm around his neck and rolled him to his back before she kissed him, tasting herself mixed with the taste of Shayne. He caressed over her back down to her bum where he spanked her with a short, snappy slap. He combed his fingers through her hair. "This is what it is, Lacey," he said in a low voice.

"But what is it?"

His gaze searched hers. "I don't know."

Neither did she. She sat up, grabbed the quilt and once more covered them. She rested her head on his chest once more. His fingers combing through her hair was soothing. He found a lost bobby pin, gently untangled it then tossed it onto the nightstand. She heard the little sound it made over the beating of his heart.

Shayne is in my bed.

It was her last thought before sleep pulled her under.

Chapter 3

WHAT THE HELL?...

The thought circled his brain like the water going down the drain. Nothing like reality the morning after.

Sex with Lacey was...

Exhaling, Shayne tilted his head back so the water rained down on his face. He had left her sleeping. He'd kissed that biteable, fuckable ass then had done the walk of shame in his tuxedo. There had been some relief to find Todd wasn't home. He did not need the razzing that would've greeted him.

How did he tell Todd he had slept with his sister?

Opening his mouth, Shayne took a mouthful of water then spat it out, hating that some of Lacey left with the water. Earlier he had collapsed on the spare bed in Todd's small townhouse, still wearing his pants. Sleep. He had needed sleep.

Because he had sure as shit not gotten any last night.

His ass was going to be dragging. The game was at three then there was the annual barbecue at Coach's house.

Shit. Coach.

What the hell was he going to say to Coach? *So, nice party last night. Fucked your firstborn's brains out. Did you know Lacey screams? Mind if I bend her over the picnic table because I'm not entirely sure I'm done with her?*

"Awesome," he sighed as he shoved his face under the water again.

Lacey.

Lacey of the sexy kisses. Lacey of the long legs. Lacey of the curious hands. Lacey of the succulent pussy. Lacey of the luscious ass.

Shayne of the swollen cock.

How the hell was going to keep his hands off Lacey after the game?

A fist hammered on the door. "You primping in there, Princess? Hurry the fuck up."

And there was the answer to the how.

Shayne turned off the shower then reached for the towel, wiping up water then wrapping it around his waist. "Girl." As he walked by Todd, he knocked into his shoulder.

"Pussy. Fucking better be hot water."

There was. Shayne's shower had been cold from beginning to end because the smell of Lacey had been all over him, leaving him hard and aching, with the driving need to return to her warm bed.

Trouble. Trouble. Trouble.

With a groan, he belly flopped onto the bed and muttered a curse into the mattress.

He did not need this. He seriously did not need this.

But oh, how he wanted this, because sex with Lacey was off-the-charts-amazing.

The hockey game had been retribution for Coach. His home team had massacred them. With the final score of six-four, Coach had simply pointed at Shayne then bobbed his eyebrows. Shayne's had been up four-one by the end of the second period then Coach's team had come to life and scored on him five times. Five! Embarrassing.

Shayne lay on the grass in Coach's backyard, blocking out the sounds of the small barbecue. "Hey, wet noodle." A foot nudged him and he grunted in response, too tired to do anything about Lacey kicking him. Or not, he decided when he grabbed her foot at the next poke and pulled it out from under her. She gave a girly shriek as she hit the ground, punching his chest.

"When did you get here?"

"Five minutes ago. Ish. We'd have been here sooner but I had to murder my child and bury her under the porch."

There was a tension in her voice that made him move his arm from over his eyes. She was still wearing her disgusting green Husks jersey. The only redeeming thing about it was the twenty-three on the back. Did it say something about it him that it made him hot as hell to know she was wearing his number?

It took all his self-control to not roll on top of her, tug down those skin-licking jeans and fuck them both into a coma. His hormones were on a rampage. He wanted Lacey naked and underneath him--now. *It's the ice*, he thought trying not to focus on the woman beside him. The ice always got him revved up, even when he lost. He supposed it was the adrenalin. Either way when he stepped off the ice, he wanted sex. He wanted sex with Lacey. Right. Now. Even though they were at her parents' house. And didn't that turn him into a sick asshole.

Hands braced behind her, she sat with her legs stretched out and her head tilted back. "You don't have a porch," said Shayne. At least he was tracking the conversation despite his obsession with getting her naked.

"Did I say I'd buried her at my house? That would be too easy. I'd immediately be a suspect when someone reported her missing. Nice turnout this year," she said, gazing around the yard.

"Mom, can I invite Chelsea? This party blows. Everyone is *old*."

Shayne shifted his arm and blinked in shock. No way was that Carmen. Carmen was thin and gawky. She looked exactly like Lacey now. Exactly. It was as if Lacey had been cloned. From the wavy dark hair, to the Magerin nose, to the whiskey eyes, to the long, willowy body, she looked just like her mother. Holy. Hell.

"Ask Gram. This isn't my house."

Carmen huffed in irritation while managing to look as if this was the worst day of her life. "I don't know why I can't have friends here."

"Ask Gram," Lacey repeated. He had the feeling this had been going on for awhile.

"This sucks," Carmen snapped and spun away. He noticed she didn't go ask her grandmother if she could invite her friend. Instead she went to go stand with Coach.

"When did she get so..." Somehow calling a fifteen year old gorgeous was wrong.

"A year ago. One day she morphed into a teenage mutant, a beautiful teenage mutant. I look at her and wonder where my baby went. Kevin, being Kevin, wants her to model. Carmen thinks that's brilliant because then she'll be famous. She's mad because I'm saying no. According to Kevin, I hold our daughter back just like I held him back." She shrugged a shoulder. "Throw in the divorce and I have one angry kid."

He curled his hand around her wrist, squeezing reassuringly. "Wake me when your dad sets the grill on fire." He covered his eyes again but continued to hold onto Lacey. He didn't sleep. It was more like he hovered between in a state of semi-consciousness. He heard familiar voices, smelled the food cooking, felt the soft skin under his hand, yet he was unaware of everyone.

Someone joined them. Female. He couldn't place the voice but didn't care enough to wake up completely to see who it was. A child's laughter, the oof from Lacey while her body moved beside his. He was aware of her hand vanishing, heard her shush what sounded like a kid.

Another voice joined them. Todd. There was the momentary panic of what would he tell Todd about lying on the grass beside his sister. He wondered how his friend would react if he had known that there had been sexy fun times with his older sister. He envisioned his dead body buried beside Carmen's under an anonymous deck.

"And there it goes," he heard Todd say.

Shayne eased his arm off his face and shifted to see

the plume of smoke rise up from the grill. Coach waved his arm back and forth.

"Dinner's ready," Lacey added. "Anyone want to go for pizza?"

It was a testament to Coach that no one raised their arm. He sat and rubbed his face with a yawn. Todd had been close-mouthed about where he had stayed the night. Both of them getting laid, neither saying a word. Fantastic. Weren't they a couple of cagey bastards?

He looked at the woman who stood up gracefully on the other side of Lacey. He knew that long blonde hair and sad blue-grey eyes. Shannon Koval. She had been at the Magerin house as much as he had until Lacey had married the asshat.

"Look at you, both in your green jerseys. Boo. Hiss," Shayne muttered. In the annual game, the visiting team wore the Husks yellow away jersey while the home team wore Husks green. In the drawing of names, Shayne had wound up as a yellow jersey with Todd and Adam Payne. The green jerseys had handed them their asses.

Carmen appeared. "Mom," she whispered, "Coach burned the hamburgers. By burned I mean they look like hockey pucks. Do I have to eat one?"

"No," Lacey whispered back. "Take one and throw it at Shayne. See if he catches it. He missed everything else thrown at him today."

"Hey," he said, wrapping an arm around Carmen's neck. "I can hear you two, you know. When did you get so tall, kid? You're supposed to feed the kid, Lacey, not put her on a rack and stretch out her legs."

"I'm the tallest girl in my class," the girl said with a

bit of a sulk. "I hate it."

"Just means you don't have to stretch as far when you reach for your dreams, baby," Lacey said.

"Well, you won't let me," Carmen snapped, her sulk returning.

Lacey looked at her daughter. Shayne saw the little flinch around her eyes. Their similarities were shocking. He wondered if he'd ever get used to see a younger version of Lacey running around. One was enough. Two was overkill. "I said you had to be sixteen and maintain good grades for a year. Neither have happened."

"You would let me model if I were Kayla."

"Had she wanted to model at fifteen, the rules would've been the same. We aren't arguing about this anymore. Keep it up and I'll make you eat one of those hamburgers."

"Pick your battles," he told the girl in a low voice. She looked at him with surprised eyes. He squeezed her shoulders and directed her to the table loaded with food. In anticipation of her husband's fantastic ability to char everything on the grill, Mrs. Magerin also provided various kinds of salad, buns and cheeses. She never served hot food because that would make Coach look like he couldn't cook.

The annual fire cloud wasn't any hint to that truth at all.

A young boy looked at a charred, shrivelled hot dog wiener then up at Shannon. "Mom," he whispered, his voice nervous and woeful all at once.

Shannon bent down to whisper in his ear while she put a bun and some fruit on his plate. She pointed at

Mrs. Magerin, who gave a wiggle of her finger. The kid was getting a decent hot dog. He knew it. Favouritism.

Lacey picked up a hamburger and tossed it lightly in her hand before she grinned. It was a bad girl grin. She spun and threw it at him. Reflex had him reaching up to catch it before it hit him in the head, knocking him unconscious.

"Good catch. Had you played like that, maybe you would've won."

She thought she was so clever.

"Good burgers this year, Coach!" Shayne called to Coach. The man lifted his hand in acknowledgement while giving Shannon's kid the evil eye when he came out of the house with a pristine and edible hot dog. Beside him Carmen giggled and he winked at her. God, he loved spending time with the Magerins.

Crouching down, Lacey focused the camera on the beer bottles being held by the two men. They sat side by side, managing to look identical despite the gulf in their ages. Neither of them spoke, they just slumped on the bench of the picnic table, this morning's hockey battle forgotten. She wanted their faces slightly blurred but recognizable. With a press of her finger, she captured the image of her dad and Todd.

Lowering her camera, she studied the two men of the Magerin clan. Man, they had some good-looking DNA. They were so much alike: the same drive and determination, the same stubborn way. If not for the arthritis that had hit him at twenty, Todd would've followed in their dad's skate grooves. Like Coach, he played left wing. Only not in the NHL but in the city's league when he wasn't running his sports bar or being flattened by pain.

Her gaze shifted to her best friend. Shannon Koval sat on the grass chatting with Jimmy, who was married to Lacey's youngest sister, Janine. Like the majority of the men around the fire, Jimmy had gone to MHS. According to Coach, Jimmy had the heart but held a stick like he was hacking weeds. Shannon's dad was a regular at family get-togethers and he sat in a chair, her son Daniel on his lap as the boy slept. She snapped a picture of the family because to not seemed like a crime.

"Don't they give you time off for good behaviour?"

It was hard to stifle the smile at the familiar voice. She looked up, camera at the ready and captured Shayne standing behind her. The sexy quirk of his mouth, the lazy, relaxed look in his eyes. All captured forever by her camera. "Who said I was good?"

"Nobody I know." He dropped down beside her and leaned back on his bent arms.

He was gorgeous and yummy. It took all her self-control to not straddle his lap and devour his mouth. He grinned then winked at her. "When she was good," he said, his head tilting back to study the night sky. "She was good. And when she was bad she was really, really good."

She snorted as she copied his position, abandoning her camera. Her gaze landed on Carmen who sat between her grandmother's legs while her hair was braided. Everyone got charming, fun Carmen. Lacey got the anger. Sometimes she could understand why she was the target.

Carmen's world had changed. Her safe little world was no longer picture perfect. Her father was living with a twenty-two year old lollipop. Her big sister was away at university. Her parents were divorced. Everyone seemed to be moving forward and she wasn't. Yes, Lacey could understand but that didn't mean she liked being the villain in Carmen's world.

Dana said something and Carmen giggled. It was a happy sound that twisted through Lacey's heart.

Everything was a battle now. Everything.

And had been since Lacey had kicked Kevin out of the house.

"Sad Lace," Shayne said quietly beside her.

She looked away from Carmen to meet the hazel eyes that were watching her. She nodded once. "Sad Lace," she agreed.

"Wanna get drunk?"

One more nod. That sounded like a brilliant idea. There were plenty of beds in her childhood home. Her old bedroom had been redone years ago for the girls so they could have sleepovers even though Lacey was about five minutes away. It wasn't the distance, but the adventure. Carmen still spent the occasional night here. Plus her daughter would get some desperately needed Grandma TLC. A lot had changed for Carmen in the past year, except this house.

Thank God. Lacey wasn't sure she could handle this home changing too.

Shayne easily rolled to his feet and held out his hand. When she put her hand in his, that almost familiar skittering sensation moved through her. He snatched up her camera then led the way inside.

Even though she had her own house, this was home.

How many breakfasts had she had at that table? How many times had she helped her mom repaint the walls? She had been there when the dishwasher went on strike, flooding the kitchen while her mother gave a "Hallelujah, I get a new dishwasher." It smelled of home. Of sweat and flowers, dinner leftovers and the dust spray her mother used.

Shayne took her into the darkened living room that always smelled of furniture polish and beeswax candles. "Hold this." He handed the camera over then opened the glass cabinet that housed bottles of wine and hard liquor. When he squatted, she admired the way the old, faded jeans stretched over his ass. "Ahh, there you are." He withdrew a bottle, took her hand then led her into the quiet family room.

Here it wasn't as formal as the dining room. Here the family lived. He yanked the cushions off the couch, dropped them on the floor then turned on the gas-powered fireplace.

It was the only light in the room. He flopped down then with a flick of his fingers removed the cap. "Can you keep up, Magerin?" He set two shot glasses on the floor. When had he pocketed those? Fast hands. He could've been a thief.

She snorted as she sank onto the other cushion. "I was drinking before you were taking slap shots, Donnelly. Can *you?*"

He filled the two glasses, then dragged his finger up the neck of the bottle. He held it out to her. Unable to resist, she leaned forward and took his finger into her mouth. He tasted of wood smoke, salt and tequila. Her tongue licked along him, over the bumps of his knuckles and then the broad tip.

"Fuck," he said then with a quick look at the doorway, he fisted his hand in her hair and kissed her.

The man did not kiss shyly. It was always bold thrusts of his tongue and hungry pulls of his mouth. He kissed like he played hockey, with all his concentration and determination. She hooked her arm behind his neck, just as greedy for his mouth.

She could run but she couldn't hide from what he had stirred in her last night.

The kiss ended as abruptly as it began. Lacey blinked, focusing on Shayne as he grabbed a shot glass and slammed back the tequila with a shudder. His gaze drifted over her face before meeting her gaze.

Unwilling to look away, she located the second glass and downed the alcohol, setting the empty glass down.

He reached over, grabbed her cushion and pulled her closer. "You are seriously sexy," he said in a low voice. "When did you become sexy, Lace?"

"Probably when you did."

His thumb stroked along her cheekbone. "I keep telling myself last night was a mistake. That I was drunk and it didn't count." Only neither of them had been drunk. His thumb moved to her lower lip and she shivered at the slow exploration while he voiced everything she had thought throughout the day. "I vowed it was a one shot deal. I promised myself that..." He lowered his head and kissed her.

He tasted of tequila and sexy male.

"And then I'd see you." His gaze looked deep into her, the colour that delicious golden hue when he was aroused. "I'd get hard and my only thought, my only want, my only wish is to be deep inside you.

"You put me off my game, Lace. I saw you circling the rink, camera snapping and whirring and I'd have flashbacks to you arched beneath me, screaming my name as you came. Next thing I know there's some asshole with the puck."

"Poor big, bad goalie." She caressed his cheek, moving to her back to see him better. Her head rested on his cushion. "Done in by a mere mortal."

He sighed as he traced her neck. "There's nothing mere about you." He took her mouth again, his hand slipping under the neck of her tee. She arched as he traced the edge of her bra. "Tell me you're wet. Tell me your panties are uncomfortably damp as they get to kiss that sweet pussy of yours. Tell me you still feel my cock filling you."

"Shayne." She could barely remember to breathe as he drew the fabric aside. Heat clenched through her when his fingers teased her nipple swollen for his touch.

"Tell me," he rasped the words out. "Tell me you want me like I want you."

She shouldn't be doing this. This was madness. This wasn't going to have a happy ending and she was tired of things ending in the shit. This was reckless and she hadn't been that way since she had been a kid and she didn't need to be a mom. This was insanity because of who they were to each other.

His thumb brushed back and forth over the tight flesh of her nipple so that she felt it in a responding touch lower down.

"Shayne." She whispered his name because it was easier to say. His jaw was covered in dark stubble and she enjoyed the rasp of the whiskers against her hand. His dark hair was soft in comparison despite the short length. Her hand curled around the back of his head and she drew him down, kissing him because she couldn't voice the arousal flowing through her for him.

His fingers pinched and pulled on her nipple as they kissed. His hand slid away and he pushed her cushion back, breaking the kiss.

She lay there, gasping for air and control while he tilted the glass and poured more tequila. Out in the hallway, she heard what he had. Footsteps.

"Fuck," she sighed wistfully and with frustration before she rolled over. No one needed to know how achingly hard her nipples were.

"I wish," Shayne muttered, glaring at the doorway. "Here's to frustration." He tapped the shot glass against hers then downed the alcohol. "You'll never make it as a spy, Magerin."

Lacey hated her brother as he came in. She downed the tequila then took control of the bottle.

"You're into Coach's booze? Oh, he's gonna be mad at you." Todd climbed over the couch, grabbed a throw pillow and joined them.

"Todd's jealous," Lacey said, "because he wasn't invited." Her brother took her glass and shot the liquid, coughing. "Sissy."

"Bitch."

She grinned because he was her brother and she loved him. Because it would annoy him, she messed up his curly hair.

"Ugh, you bitch. I paid seven dollars for this trim." He smoothed a hand down his hair. "What are we up to?"

"Two."

"Sweet." He grabbed Shayne's glass and downed it. "Now we're even. Rack 'em up, toots."

"Go get your own glass. And see if there are any cookies," Shayne said. "Fucking love some chocolate chip."

"Assholes everywhere." Todd rolled to his feet and went to play fetch.

Lacey planted her hands on the floor and pushed herself forward. Fortified with a little more alcohol in her system, she put her mouth against Shayne's ear. "I'm wet," she whispered. "My panties are uncomfortably damp as they stick to a pussy that still feels you hours later. I want, Shayne. I want." She bit his earlobe and dropped back into her original position. A shaky exhale came from him as a low moan.

They stared at each other. Arousal burned in his gaze.

She wanted to go home. She wanted him to come with her. Her body remembered his hands on her, caressing everywhere as he explored. Her body remembered and because of that it hungered for more. He picked up her camera and she was shocked when he took her picture. "Now you'll see," he said, "what I see."

Todd returned with a plate of leftover cookies and Lacey willed her arousal to subside.

"Ahh, excellent," Shayne said as he took a cookie. "I've been craving something sweet in my mouth."

62

Chapter 4

THERE WERE HANGOVERS. And then hangovers on hardwood floors.

She was too old for this. That was her only thought as she opened her eyes to stare at the ceiling. There was a heavy arm on her stomach and a warm hand buried in her panties. He slept on his stomach, his face buried in her neck as he snored. After they had killed the bottle of tequila, her brother had started to nod off and only a nudge from her had him looking for a bed.

As soon as he had left, Shayne had been on her like water. They hadn't gotten naked. That was good. She'd hate to be naked on the floor in her parents' house, but God had he made her come with his hand and his mouth whispering every little naughty thing he wanted to do with her.

She caressed his arm then gently pulled his hand out of her pants. She sat up with a groan then zipped up her jeans. Her head hurt and her body ached. Tequila was a vengeful bitch.

There was a vague memory of saying goodnight to Carmen who had gawked at her mother and uncle drinking on the floor like a couple of idiots. Stellar mothering there. Sometime after midnight, her parents had come in and said good-night as if the three of them hadn't been piss-drunk. They had made her laugh, Shayne and Todd. She couldn't remember the last time she had laughed like that.

Or cried. She remembered crying against Todd's chest.

She ventured into the half-bathroom on the first floor and shuddered when she saw her hangover face. Whisker burns. Awesome.

She readjusted her bra and washed her face with cold water, holding a cloth against her feverish skin. Leaning against the wall, Lacey sighed. Again the crazy thought raced through her mind.

What was she doing?

Fooling around with Shayne was dangerous. So many people could get hurt by this.

She folded the damp cloth and hung it on the holder then made her way upstairs for the shower. She was sticky between her legs and she felt as if a train had hit her. She had passed out on the floor.

With Shayne's hand in her pants.

Where anyone could see. Her mom. Her dad. Her brother. Her daughter.

Brilliant. Yeah, she was smart.

She showered and began to feel human. There were whisker burns on her breasts.

And a hickey.

She traced it, trying to remember him sucking on the skin that hard. A lot was a blur from the time he had pounced on her until she had woken up. Tequila haze. A glorious thing.

The thought of getting back into her clothes depressed her. The panties she stuffed into the front pocket of her jeans and she winced at the denim on her bare skin. How embarrassing.

"Idiot," she told her reflection as she combed out her hair. Upon exiting the washroom, she smelled the most heavenly scent. First she made a detour into her old bedroom. Her daughter looked so young as she slept, curled on her side, hand gripping the corner of her pillow. Her unhappy, hurting, beautiful child. Lacey brushed aside the dark brown hair. "I do love you, Carmen," she whispered as she kissed her forehead, "no matter what you think."

She left her daughter sleeping, venturing downstairs.

"Coffee," she breathed the word like the blessing it was.

She followed the scent to see her father standing at the fridge. He wore a faded Winnipeg Jets t-shirt with his grubby khaki pants. She poured herself a mug of coffee and leaned against the counter. "I can't believe Mom hasn't thrown that out." The t-shirt had to be at least as old as Carmen, since the team had moved to Phoenix in '96. There was a hole under the left armpit.

"She tries. Morning, baby." Coach kissed her cheek. "Omelet?"

The thought of her father's cooking this early in the day made her hung-over stomach roll. "I'm fine. Thanks."

He gave her a beady eye and she tried to look innocent.

"Heard you crying last night."

Shit. Had he heard her later with Shayne? "Sorry. Tequila haze."

He cracked an egg like it was his enemy then muttered curses as he removed shell from the bowl. "Heard you laugh too. Good to hear that sound." He smashed the hell out of a second egg and she felt sorry for the poor little things. They had no idea the suffering they'd have at the hands of Roger Magerin. He grabbed a whisk and beat the eggs, murdering the wee beasties. He set the bowl aside and she watched him hack up back bacon like he was psycho.

It was brutal watching what he did to some green peppers and cheese.

She swore the mixture screamed in pain when he dumped everything into the frying pan, begging for mercy. It was an unholy mess on his plate and he added more back bacon. Her mother would kill him if she knew how much bacon was on that plate, let alone the salt.

"The boys took care of you last night?"

Boys? Fuck. "No. I stripped naked and ran up and down the street, yelling 'Go Steam Go!' " Her father glared at her, not because she mentioned Shayne's NHL team but for her sarcasm, as he picked up his knife and sawed his omelet.

And sawed.

And sawed.

God love her father, he was a horrific cook.

"Sweet baby Jesus, what is that?"

She glanced at the doorway at the startled cry and

saw Shayne was looking at Coach's plate with what could only be described as disgusted horror. His hair was wet and he had shaved. Where had he found a razor? Like her, he wore last night's clothes. Unlike her, she bet he was still wearing his shorts. Jerk.

"Wise ass. Both of you." Coach pointed his knife at Shayne then at her.

Lacey batted her eyes innocently then drew a circle around her head like a halo. Shayne snorted as he passed by her to help himself to coffee. He leaned against the counter beside her, smelling of soap and man. She wanted to rub against him and climb him so she could kiss that mouth.

Lacey set her mug down and eased away from Shayne. "I need clothes that don't smell like smoke." She kissed her dad's cheek. "It was a fantastic barbecue, Dad. And way to kick their ass yesterday. Bring Carm home whenever you'd like."

"Bye, baby." He patted her shoulder then returned to tackling his, for a lack of a better word, breakfast. She retrieved her camera, found her purse in the living room then headed out to her car.

The knock on the passenger window made her heart stutter. *Don't do it. Don't unlock that door.* She hit the button and Shayne slid into the seat beside her.

"This is not smart," she said, nervously. God, he made her so...nervous. Giddy. Hot.

"Drive. Told your dad I was going to snag a ride to Todd's. Something about hangovers, floors, and his breakfast."

Lacey licked her upper lip as she thought of a million

reasons why this was a bad idea.

"I swear to God, Lacey, if you don't get out of this driveway, I'm going to fuck you right here. Drive."

She drove.

Never had she been so aware of another person in her life. His breathing was a little heavy, his hair was already beginning to dry while hers was still damp. Like her clothes, the smell of wood smoke drifted from his. She saw his hand curl into a fist then slowly ease open one finger at a time, a man strangling his control. He was the one who opened the glove compartment and removed the remote, opening her garage.

"Get. Out." His voice was low and raspy and she flicked a glance at him. His jaw was clenched, his eyes closed.

Her hand shook as she opened the door then walked to the door. Her heart sounded loud in her ears. Louder than his door slamming shut behind him. The clatter of her keys on the hall table sounded like a gunshot. The thump of her purse on the floor sounded muffled. A hand grabbed her wrist and she was yanked back and turned.

Heat.

That's all there was.

Heat.

His mouth claimed hers with hunger, his tongue licking and teasing hers as he drew her shirt up, breaking contact long enough to fling it towards the living room. "Fuck." He dragged her into him as he backed her towards her room, his hands battling with her bra. "This thing is..."

She pushed up his shirt and he was the one who

yanked it off, dropping it behind him. She was the one who released the clasp of her bra. He was the one who ripped it off then slammed her hard against the wall.

"Smelled you all night." His hands slid down her arms, caught her wrists then pinned her hands above her head. "The smell of your skin," he lowered his head and inhaled along her neck. "Your hair. Your orgasms. Fuck, your orgasms, Lace."

She could only pant as his hands caressed down her arms, every finger leaving a blazing trail.

"Your clothes. I tasted you all night." He rested his forehead against hers so she had no choice but to gaze into eyes turned golden with arousal. "Tasted you on my tongue so there was no tequila left. Tasted you on my lips until I thought I'd lick them raw. The feel of you against me, all night." He groaned, his eyes closing. "All night. Was hard all night. Hurting for you. I knew when you were gone, Lacey."

Shayne's eyes opened and her breath caught in her throat. Dear God. His fingers lightly caressed her waist while he looked at her with such passion it left her feeling weak.

She lowered her hands so her wrists rested on her head lacking the strength to hold her arms up anymore. Lacey couldn't look away as he slowly unbuttoned her jeans then slid the zipper down.

"You're not wearing panties."

She shook her head then gasped as his hand slid into the parted vee of her jeans. His fingers searched for the slickness of her pussy.

"You're not wearing..." his voice faded as he shut his

eyes, swallowed then caressed over her hip and down her ass.

He yanked her hips into his as he ravaged her mouth with another one of his searing kisses. Fingers squeezed and caressed, rocking her against the heavy bulge behind his jeans. His other hand tugged on the side of her jeans. It wasn't graceful. It was a jerky move that was sexier in its lack of coordination. This man who could nab a puck out of the air was yanking sporadically on her jeans until the waistband was past her hips.

He growled as he palmed her other ass cheek in his hand and pinned her between the wall and his hard body. His hips rolled forward, his erection rubbing and rubbing, his hands squeezing and squeezing.

"Shayne." She grabbed his hips, rising up on her toes so he hit her...right...there. "Oh, God, Shayne."

"Fucking in you," he snarled as he slammed hard against her, driving her into the wall. "In you now."

Her knees buckled and she found herself on the floor, two hundred pounds of aroused male surging against her. Her jeans hampered her movement. He was dressed. She wanted to feel him inside her. Needed it like most people needed water. He pushed off her long enough to rip her jeans away and then with a groan he was back.

Her legs hooked over his thighs as she cried out against the rub of denim, the scrape of button over her clit. His kisses were addicting. It was the lack of control, the onslaught of hunger that left her breathless. She didn't want polite, sweet kisses because that wasn't who he was.

He was raw and savage and untamed.

She liked that he was so aroused by her he had no control. She felt his hand between them as he battled his fly and she gripped the back pockets of his jeans as she watched this man above her. With a grunt, he gripped her ass and slammed hard into her.

Hard enough to scoot her on the floor. Hard enough to make her cry out. Hard enough to make her see stars.

Sex with Kevin had never been about this. About passion and desire and greedy need.

"Oh God," she moaned as she felt the full flesh slide within her, driving thrusts in and almost slow retreats as if he didn't want to leave her. She caressed up the shifting muscles of his back. God, he was strong. It was sexy how strong he was. Curious, she dragged her hand down, scratching along his spine.

He arched up from her, his hips plunging hard against hers, while he hissed. His eyes opened and his smile was sinful. A brawny arm was braced above her head as he tried to rein in the fierce thrusts.

"Don't," she pleaded as she slid her hands under the loose jeans to the smooth, warm flesh of his ass. "Don't hold back on me. Don't."

"Want it to last."

She shook her head. "Don't hold back. Don't."

Fingers dug into her ass and he dragged her closer. "Then I won't." And he didn't. He took her hard on the floor, every slap of his body against hers making her cry out. "Come, Lace. Want to feel you come."

"Yes." She gripped his hips and met those deliciously erotic strikes of his body.

"Come for me, baby. Let go and come. God, you're

wet." He grabbed her thigh, hiking her leg up higher on his hip. "Sucking against my cock, so wet. And hot. God, you're steamy. Come for me. Fuck me and come." His hand was gentle despite his words and thrusts. "Want to feel this sweet pussy squeeze me as you arch up and..."

She bowed up and he hissed a yes in her ear as she came. A muffled sound came from him before he gave one, hard final thrust and buried himself in her. She felt the warm silky spurts as he came in her, his hand squeezing her ass. He held her against him as little jerks came from him.

He sank onto her, heavy and sweaty and so delicious. A shift of his head and he was kissing her with a drugging intensity. "Lacey," he whispered as he buried his face in her neck, rolling her so she lay on him. He slipped from her, his cock lubed from both of them.

No condom.

Two more terrifying words in the world she didn't know. He was soft and damp against her thigh. She rested her cheek on his chest and heard the frantic thumps of his heart.

"I came in you." The words were spoken slowly and dazed.

She nodded.

"I've never..." He cupped her hips then eased her off of him. A curse escaped him and he sat up, his gaze landing on the damp spot on her floor.

To see such a confident man this bewildered was a little scary. No thoughts of birth control had entered her mind. That was logical and nothing that had happened since the other night was logical. "Shayne?" She touched his tattooed wrist and felt him flinch as if she had lashed him.

"Never," he repeated in a low whisper. His head lifted and he looked shattered. "I have to..." He looked around, so lost her heart hurt. *This* was the boy she remembered. "Go." He nodded as he once more looked at that damp spot. "Go," he whispered.

It was painful to watch him slowly get to his feet. His hands were shaking. He had the sturdiest hands. He zipped his jeans then stood there. Lost. She knelt on the floor, her thighs sticky from their orgasms, and watched him unravel before her.

He recognized his shirt and picked it up. He looked at it like he didn't know what it was for. *Oh Shayne.*

A harsh exhale came from him. "I'll call." And he left.

The front door quietly clicked behind him and she stayed on the floor for a long time, tears sliding down her cheeks.

Chapter 5

SHAYNE ROLLED THE puck back and forth before him, yesterday morning replaying through his mind like a scratched record.

There was one fundamental truth: he had come inside Lacey.

Fuck, she'd felt good. Slick and warm, wet and welcome. Never in his entire sexual life had he gone without a condom. First because he hadn't wanted to knock up some girl and wind up stuck in Granville, his dreams of the big league in ashes. Then once he made it onto an NHL team it had been because he'd be damned if someone would wave a paternity paper in his face.

He didn't want kids. Ever.

He had come inside Lacey.

Tapping the black puck, he watched it roll until he stopped it with his other hand. Back and forth it went.

"This is a surprise."

Putting two fingers on the puck, he halted its motion and watched Lacey enter the small office that was hers inside the arena. Framed photos were on the walls. Pictures she had taken. Some were of the girls, some of her family, some of MHS. A collection of yearbooks was on a bookshelf. Yearbooks filled with her photos.

She had left modelling after a few years and had found herself behind the camera. He recalled it had started as a hobby. But she was good. She was really, really good. Some big name hockey players called her for photos because she had this way of taking a picture that made one feel as if he was in the middle of the game.

"I couldn't stay at Todd's. Too many thoughts." And all of them contradicted each other.

Shayne stared at the Husks logo on the puck because it was easier to look at than Lacey. That didn't stop him from being aware of her setting a fancy camera on her desk or walking back and shutting her office door with a loud click. She sat on the edge of her desk not far from his hand. Damn her, she was wearing a little denim skirt that flashed miles of leg.

Okay, honestly it ended at her knees but it was still too short.

He was in hell and he wanted to lower his head to her lap while exploring all that bare leg. His brain was in turmoil and his body was all *Ooh, Lacey playground. Can we play, huh huh? Can we?*

With an exhausted sigh, he leaned back in the chair and looked up at Lacey. Yes, she was beautiful. There was no denying the truth. There was also something reassuring in the way she watched him with cognac eyes looking soft and understanding. Even if the woman weren't Lacey, he'd still be sitting here. Todd was his best friend but he couldn't imagine sitting before him like this, feeling raw and vulnerable. He hated that word.

Vulnerable.

It was so victim sounding. He was no victim.

His hand squeezed the puck. Six ounces of vulcanized rubber. His thumb rubbed over the rough edge then the smooth face where he traced the logo. It was the singular most consistent object in Shayne's life. It never changed, was never improved. It was perfection and you couldn't improve on that. "I don't want kids, Lace." His gaze bounced up to hers before returning to the puck. "Ever."

"I figured."

"I should get a vasectomy. Every time I book it though, something happens. But the women I fuck, I wouldn't exactly want to dip my dick into them unprotected."

A little laugh escaped her. "Never boff the bunnies, Shayne."

He shrugged. He had no excuse for sleeping with the hockey chasers. They were there. They were handy. It was sex. Just sex. He didn't do relationships. They came with expectations and promises. Donnellys didn't do expectations or promises.

"I've never," he exhaled, breaking up his thought. Leaning forward he set the puck back on her desk then looked up at her. "I never wanted to go bareback. Ever. All it takes is one determined sperm and everything changes. I didn't want to be stuck here. I would've been stuck here. Am I shallow? I'm shallow. Once I left Granville I didn't want a kid to hold me back. Then once I became really good, I didn't want a kid to be a hostage negotiation for money. Always condoms. *Always*. Only mine, never hers because there's sabotage: a pin, a fingernail, old condoms. *Always*." He met her steady gaze. "Until you."

With a groan, he dropped his head to her thigh because he needed physical contact and he was exhausted. Her hand smoothed along his hair. The touch was soothing and reassuring. "I told myself earlier that that was it. No more fucking around with Lacey Magerin. And yet here I am." He was confused. She confused the hell out of him. Every sign he saw told him to stay away from her and yet here he was.

She had Granville permanently tattooed on her soul and the thought of him coming back here where he was always Jerry Donnelly's kid made his skin tight. People who remembered his dad, didn't look at Shayne and say "That's Shayne Donnelly, he's in the NHL now." No, they said, "That's Jerry Donnelly's kid."

She had ventured out into the big, bad world but had returned. Permanently.

He came back sporadically. In the ten years since he had left, he could count his flights into Regina on one hand. His one and only goal had been to get the fuck out of Granville. If it hadn't been hockey, he would've hit the highway with his thumb pointing in any direction.

He was, as Adam Payne said, a dirt farm boy. The only thing his father had grown on that small plot of land had been dirt, hangovers and bruises. Nothing thrived in that shack, not even Shayne. There were times even now when he woke up half expecting to see old hand-me-downs, a black eye and dirt on his skin.

And here he was, fooling around with Coach's daughter.

What a piece of shit he was.

The Magerins had been good to him. He couldn't keep track of the amount of meals Mrs. Magerin had fed him or the times he'd slept over or the hours spent on the ice with Coach and Todd. He was Jerry Donnelly's kid, she was Roger Magerin's daughter. He was dirt, she was gold.

"What are you doing with me?" he asked softly, not really aware of voicing the question out loud.

A surprised laugh escaped her, quiet and low. "I have *no* idea, Shayne. Saturday morning I woke up and went with my mom to the salon for a style and a pedicure. Saturday afternoon I got into a screaming match with Carmen. Saturday evening I was remembering the last function where Kevin was my date and how so much could change in a year. Then I turn and there's this guy who isn't the kid I remember making me think things I shouldn't. Saturday night I'm naked in my bed with him. Trust me when I say I have no idea what I'm doing."

He ran his hand down her leg. She had the silkiest skin. Head to toe. How cliché but it was true. His fingers traced the graceful curve of her calf, her slender ankle wrapped in leather straps from her sandals then back up to her knee then down again.

"For the record, I don't want a baby either. Jesus, my oldest is nineteen. At nineteen I was married. That's old enough to make me a grandma and if she's carrying around a baby sibling, the world will assume it's hers. Fuck, the fifteen-year-old is old enough to make me a grandma. A baby wouldn't be fair to the girls. I'll be honest, I debated the morning after pill. My life is a mess, Shayne. My kids are pissed that I kicked out their dad. How mad would they be if I said I was pregnant?"

"And yet here you are."

"Here I am," she repeated in a softer voice. "I have no idea what I'm doing with you, Shayne. Is my ego so trashed that I need to sleep with a twenty-nine year old?"

"I'm irresistible." He grinned and kissed her knee. "It's okay. Many women have succumbed to me."

She snorted then smacked his ear. "Ass."

He fell serious again as his hand slid back down so his fingers curled around her ankle. "I have to say, though, that coming in you was one of the singular sexiest moments of my life and I want to do it again and again and again." He stood up, his fingers gliding up her leg, and kissed her. Her legs parted for him and he drew her closer to the edge of the desk.

A soft, breathy sound filled his mouth as their tongues met. "And I want to feel every inch of you squeezing me as you come again and again and again." His hands followed the slender lines of her thighs, pushing the skirt up. "Sexiest feeling in the world is the sensation of you coming, Lacey. I loved coming in you." His voice was raspy at the memory of her slick skin kissing his, at the snug, heated fit of her.

"Yes," she breathed.

"So I can tell myself it was wrong until the sun grows dim but fuck do I want to do it again." His hand slid along the panties she wore and found the damp swatch. She cried out and he groaned. "Fuck, you're wet." He stroked along the fabric that was so slick he could feel the sexy lines of her pussy. "Why are you so wet for me, Lace?"

Wetness soaked through to his finger and she leaned back on her desk as she rocked against him. "Don't know," she said. "Never like this."

"No?" He smiled when she shook her head. "Poor baby." His fingers slipped under her panties and another ragged cry escaped from her. She was warm and slick, her clit a hard knot of arousal. Against the flimsy t-shirt, her nipples pressed out. His free hand gripped the back of her neck and he covered her mouth with his as he pushed two fingers into her.

She cried out as she came, shuddering gently while satiny cream spilled around his fingers.

All those lectures about staying away from her dissolved. Or had they evaporated when he found himself pulling into the parking lot of the arena, eying the building that had started it all?

Her legs hooked around his thighs as her body rolled as if to take him deeper into her. He wanted in her. His body hummed with the desperation to take what was his.

His?

"Shayne. Oh God, Shayne, there."

Fuck yes, he thought as his fingers stroked over the spot that made her say his name like that. He watched as her head fell back, dark hair falling to the desk as her hips lifted off the wood, grinding over his fingers as he worshipped that hot, wet spot within her. A foot moved to his hip for leverage. Jesus.

"Come, baby. Come."

"Shayne. Holy. God. Shayne."

His thumb brushed her clit and her body twisted to the right, her pussy squeezing his fingers. Get. In. Her. Now.

She cried out, her body freezing as muscles clamped on his fingers. She came in a rush of cream over his fingers, her body trembling from her orgasm.

Fuck. Fuck, fuck fuck.

He grabbed her, dragging and flipping her so she was bent over her desk. Her panties were drenched all along the back as he skimmed them down her legs. Her thighs were slick from her climax and her ass was a tempting globe before him.

Perfection was her ass.

His hand slid along her swollen pussy and a little jerk moved through her even as he drew the moisture still trickling from her along that little patch of skin then to her ass. His finger was slick enough from her orgasm that it easily slid into the tiny hole. Her hand slapped against the desk, curling over the opposite edge.

Was he doing this?

Could he not?

His free hand fumbled with his jeans as he watched, hypnotized by the way his finger vanished into her, the little push back of her body when he eased out. He had purposefully left condoms behind so he didn't wind up doing exactly this.

A foot slid beside hers and he edged her feet further apart. "Does it hurt?" Her head shook negatively even as her hips rocked back. A finger brushed over her pussy to test her answer. "Condom?" The question rasped his throat as he asked because he knew the answer, damn it.

Another shake of her head and he cleared his throat. "Want me to stop?"

"No. Don't stop," she pleaded.

He eased his finger from the cinch of tight muscles and caressed over her ass, down her thigh then around to her abdomen. "Don't come yet," he ordered, because if she did they were repeating yesterday's mishap.

Slowly, oh so slowly because he was aware this was a dangerous place for him to be, he easily slid his cock into the wet, welcome kiss of her body. "Jesus," he whispered, and gripped the desk to keep himself from fucking hard and fast to empty into her.

"Shayne."

"Don't. Come. Please." His hips flexed forward and he felt sweat slide down his back. Pulling out of her was the hardest thing to do. "Relax," he said, clearing his throat.

"Why?"

"Just...relax." He dipped his fingers into the honeyed core of her then traced that tempting little circle.

"Shayne?"

"Want me to stop?"

Her head shook negatively for the third time and he set the head of his cock, glistening with her cream, at that entrance. He felt her still and he held his breath as he eased his way into her. Fuck.

Oh hell, she was tight.

"Don't move." Or he was going to erupt all over the most perfect ass in the world. The tight muscle gave and the head of him stretched her. He stared, mesmerized to see him breaching her ass. "God, I wish you could see."

"See what?"

"Perfection," he sighed as he resumed the slow glide into her. He heard her ragged breaths, felt the quiver of her muscles and he memorized every reaction she had. That little moan in her throat, the flexing of her fingers, the tiny push back of her hips. "Sweet God, Lacey."

It was like a switch had been flipped and he slid deep into her until the soft curves of her ass met his body. If he moved, he was going to come. Instantly. She was tighter than a fist, squeezing him until he felt massive inside her. He caressed along her arm, his fingers entwining with hers. "One more inch," he whispered in her ear. "I'm a heartbeat away from filling your ass with cum so let's just...breathe."

A hand caressed his flank and he moaned. "Don't do that. God, don't do that."

"I don't want to breathe," she said in a low, husky tone that made the skin on his spine shiver. "I want," she swallowed as he eased an inch back then pressed forward, "you."

"Look at me."

She rested her cheek on her desk. Her eyes were glazed with arousal, pupils dilated so only a bronze millimetre was visible. "I feel your heart racing with mine."

He slid his hand over the neatly trimmed dark curls and teased the glossy clit. A ragged groan came from her and the muscles in her ass tightened. "For the record, this has never happened."

"What?"

"This." A push of his hips into her buttocks had him

coming. He caught her mouth as he caressed her clit until she was coming with him. Warm rain spilled over his fingers as her ass greedily squeezed him as if to drain every drop from him. "You murder my control, Lacey."

He wanted to stay like this. A breath away from her, that luscious ass pressing into him. Reaching over, he brushed her hair out of her face so he could see her closed eyes and knowing little smile. "Sixty-seven," he said softly.

"Sixty-six," she corrected. "This morning was an inch."

Yes, he thought. Yes, it was. "I like skirts. Wear them all the time." She grinned then sighed.

"I like you in me, Donnelly."

He caressed her hip as it was really the only thing reachable unless he wanted to start up the fires again. "I like being in you, Magerin. You got tissues in here?"

"Over there." She waved a hand and he lifted his head long enough to look around her office.

Too far. He lowered his head. "I'm wrecked." He kissed her and eased out of her. Shayne grabbed the box from the shelf then dragged a chair over to where she still lay face down on her desk. He traced the slight bruising on her ass from his penetration then leaned forward to kiss the spot he had spanked the other night. She had such a delicious ass and it was all his. He wiped her thighs then over her swollen sex then drew her onto his lap.

She was limp as she sprawled on him. "Can you promise not to touch me tomorrow?"

He lowered his mouth and kissed her shoulder. Leaving his lips against her skin, he exhaled a sigh. "My flight is at seven tomorrow night." There was a subtle tensing in her body. Five days was usually more than enough time for him in Granville.

He caressed down her arm and toyed with her fingers. There was nothing pressing him to get back to Houston, it was just this place. Each of his short returns here made him feel like prey trapped in the embrace of a python, as if his very breath was being squeezed out of him one inch at a time.

His pressed their palms together and studied the difference in their hands. He felt like a Neanderthal next to her elegant hands. They were both quiet.

"You could stay a little longer." Her voice was hesitant and unsure, very un-Lacey-like.

His lips moved against her hair as he spoke. "I could." He spread his hand and slid his fingers between hers and watched as she folded hers.

"It would be a shame to miss the wheat festival."

He smiled. "It would. All that wheat."

"They have fireworks at the gravel pit."

He folded their arms so they lay on her stomach. "I like fireworks." This was the most unexpected conversation of his life. He pressed his mouth against her neck and smelled the sensual perfume she was wearing. "Do you want me to stay?"

"Yes," she whispered.

"Todd will have questions. He knows why I don't stay here. Why I can't." He should go tomorrow. Pack his padding up and go. That he was pondering staying told him this was a bad idea. Twenty-eight hours or two weeks, it would end with Lacey. He wouldn't stay and she wouldn't leave. There was no happy ending here.

"Do you want to stay?"

His lips glided up to her jaw and light kisses took him to her ear. "Yes," he whispered. Damn them both, but he wanted to stay. He wanted more minutes with her. More fool him.

Dumb fucking answer but it was the only one he had. His thumb caressed along the outside of hers and along the lower curve of her breast.

Her phone rang, an inconvenient intrusion. She eased forward to answer. "Lacey Magerin." She cleared her throat at her husky voice and he smiled as he drew his hand down her back. "Hi, baby. No, I'm fine."

"Fine, so fine," he muttered as he bunched up the pale yellow fabric of her blouse and explored the small of her back until he found the little zipper hidden at her hip. He eased it down and enjoyed the way the denim gaped open.

"It was good. Home team won. We kicked ass, including Uncle Todd's and Shayne's. You missed a good game. We also beat Coach and G in air hockey."

The conversation told him it was Kayla on the other end.

"Shayne. He was okay." She laughed and it sounded a little nervous as his hand followed the loose waist of her skirt.

What was it about Lacey that was so touchable?

A tiny shiver moved through her as his hand wandered around to her stomach and up to the underwire of her bra. She shifted on his leg, a rocking of her hips, but she didn't swat away his hand.

He tuned out the idle chitchat as he hooked his finger in the gap between her breasts then thumbed open the front clasp. The fabric fell away as a quivering breath escaped her. He leaned forward and kissed the back of her neck as he filled his palms with her breasts. Even her tits were exquisite.

Full and soft, the tips plump and hard. Her words became monosyllabic yeses and nos. Shayne grinned as he explored her with his hands. His tongue found the pulse pumping at the base of her neck while his fingers lightly pulled on her nipples. The tug seemed to cause her hips to roll. A hand landed on his knee, gripping hard.

But she didn't stop him.

"Okay. See you soon, baby. Love you. Bye." The phone bounced on the cradle then to the desk. "Asshole."

His laugh was a little wicked as he pinched the swollen tips until she cried out and her back arched. "That the best you can do?"

"No." She shifted, spreading her leg over his other one then pushed back so the wet flesh of her pussy kissed the length of his cock. "This is."

"Fuck."

Her responding laugh was more wicked then his had been as she proceeded to tease him when all he wanted was to bury himself in her again and again.

Chapter 6

PHOTOGRAPHS WERE SCATTERED everywhere. Lacey sat on the floor, contemplating an old photo that was forty years old. Or a little younger. It was hard to tell since the photographer hadn't dated the back. Jerk. If it were a little more focused she'd use it in the MHS yearbook. Her dad's back was to the camera as he stood at centre ice, a hockey stick held like a sceptre as a bunch of boys sat on the ice.

Tossing it aside, she continued to root through the photos. She loved incorporating old pictures with each yearbook. One picture made her grin even as the front door crashed open then slammed shut. The 5' 7" thunderstorm was home.

Carmen exploded into the living room and glared at Lacey. "I wanted to watch TV."

"So watch." In the photo, Carmen was six and wearing a Husks jersey with the pink pants she had loved so much because of the yellow butterfly on the knee. Little pink skates decorated her feet.

"This place is a dump. Where am I supposed to sit?"

She stood between Coach's legs, a whistle perched between lips spread in a huge grin as if she was so happy she couldn't blow. God, her baby looked small with an arm hooked behind Coach's leg. "Look how small you were." And happy. She flipped the picture around so Carmen could see it.

"Barely to Coach's knees without skates. God, you were tiny." Her five and half pound of wonder who had looked so small in her arms. "Now look at you. Ten feet of leg."

"I remember this," Carmen said softly, taking the photo, her finger on the picture. "I was assistant coach. I liked blowing the whistle when they were doing ice sprints." She smiled before it vanished. A quicksilver grin.

Her baby was so unhappy. It was killing her. Kayla was handling the divorce better than Carmen. That or being away made it easier on her. Carmen was right in the middle of the battleground.

"How come Kayla's not in the picture?"

"She was in school." Lacey settled back against the couch. Carmen rested a knee on the cushion as she stared at the picture. "You didn't have school that day. We had a day to ourselves. We went to see Coach for a few hours before we went shopping for shoes."

"I don't remember that. I wanted to go to Coach's school."

"I know." Every morning for a week, Lacey would wake up to see her baby girl sitting at the kitchen table with her skates and little Magerin hockey jersey, ready to go to hockey school. Dad would've taken her despite that girls hockey hadn't been that big when Carmen had been a kid. Kevin, though, had been adamant that his daughter wasn't going to play hockey. Lacey had to be the one to break the news to her. Carmen had screamed and thrown a skate at her then gone to Kevin.

What had her husband done next? Told her that her mom was mean but girls didn't play hockey. Asshole.

Girls went to MHS now. The teams were co-ed until middle school.

"You still can."

Carmen snorted. "Right. Like you'll let that happen."

Fuck, she was tired of being the villain in Carmen-land. Lacey tossed the pictures aside and stood up. "I am not the bad guy here, Carmen." It was too late to fight but that was pretty much all they did nowadays.

"You didn't let me go to MHS, you won't let me model, you kicked Dad out. Yeah, Mom, you're the super parent."

Lacey held up her hand and walked away. *Walk away, Lacey, and do not crush her illusions.* In her room, she closed the door. Bracing her hands on the wood, she struggled for control. Down the hall Carmen slammed her own door.

Damn it. Damn it, damn it, damn it. She thumped one fist on the door and pushed away. Her hands were shaking.

How had they come to this?

Every day was a new fight. Or an old one. Meanwhile Kevin could do no wrong as he shared a fancy condo with his lollipop. And Lacey got to hear how great and cool Amber was from her daughter. Carmen took after

Kevin in one aspect. She sure knew how to wound with her words.

Once more she heard Carmen's door slam then the front door a few minutes later. Sighing in exhaustion, Lacey flung herself onto her bed like she used to do when she was Carmen's age and angry for whatever reason. A scream of frustration came from her and she kicked the air.

Why did God invent teenagers?

What had she possibly done to warrant this kind of punishment? Was it because she had snuck out when she was seventeen to see Lyle Thompson's shiny new tractor and would've surrendered her virginity to him if he hadn't invited Donna Simmons, now Thompson, the same night? Was it because she and Shannon would lie about their whereabouts and join the other kids at the gravel pit for too much beer? Maybe because her mom wouldn't buy her those chunky earrings so she had pocketed them from the store. Or maybe she had been an axe murderer in a previous life and this was karma.

Lacey heaved a sigh. "Fuck."

Feeling a tad better, she sat up and decided she was not going to ponder the goings on in her angry daughter's head. If she stayed in solitary confinement, she'd go nuts.

She stripped off her clothes, pulled out a pair of jeans and a button top. Muttering, she wrestled with her boots, dragged a brush through her hair, grabbed her purse and went to the Penalty Box.

When all else fails, seek brother for free booze and food and a sympathetic shoulder.

The brat had to be good for something.

The Penalty Box would've been a dive in a past life. Her brother didn't believe in prettying things up. "This is where you come to drink beer and curse at refs, Mom, it's not the country club," was his monthly argument whenever their mom swept in and bemoaned the neon beer signs on the wall.

There was a pool table that had seen its fair share of fistfights. There used to be a dart board until one night someone had been so mad at Todd, he had thrown darts at him. The next night, her brother had walked in, slapped a plastic gun that shot orange plastic darts on a table and told the guy to work on his aim. There were now at least ten plastic guns in the bar.

During playoffs, the majority of the darts would be decorating one of the five televisions. Not the big screen. God help anyone if they messed up Todd's big screen baby. There was a jukebox that hadn't worked since it had been body checked by a couple of drunk MHS players. There had been a karaoke machine until Todd had set it on fire when their sisters came in night after night to sing New Kids on the Block songs.

Hockey sticks were nailed to the wall with no consideration to the autographs on the blades. Jerseys looked like ghosts in the glass cabinets and the wait staff wore black and white striped shirts like referees. There were two kinds of wine: red and white of whatever he could get the cheapest, a vast collection of draft beer, and if you came in and ordered a cocktail, he poured water and stuck an umbrella in the glass.

One would assume he hadn't grown up with five women.

The food, however, was incomparable in Granville. Yeah, the grub wasn't that complex but it was frickin' delicious. Every year, she gained five pounds during the playoffs from the beer and nachos. Those damn nachos.

Six kinds of cheese, tomatoes, jalapeños and peppered bacon.

The bastard.

He was behind the bar as usual, his hair a curly disaster as he manned the taps. He spotted her and his eyebrows rose while he plucked up a glass, tossing it like he was in the movie Cocktail. A pretzel was tucked in the corner of his mouth as he drew a beer for her.

"Carm?"

She nodded as she picked up her glass, not acknowledging him as she went to a booth. She dropped onto the bench seat, tossing her purse onto the floor. Naturally the hockey channel was on, showing a replay of an old game.

A few minutes later, Todd flung himself on the other bench, a huge beer mug filled with water. "Need an alibi?"

"No." She bent her leg and sipped her beer. She had no idea what it was and she didn't really care. She'd prefer a good scotch but he made her pay for those. For her the beer was free. "You know how Mom was always screaming at us that one day we'd get our comeuppance?"

Todd nodded as he clasped his hands behind his head. "Is Carmen your comeuppance?"

She remembered the time she had shoved Shelley's head in the toilet because she had used Lacey's brand new lipstick. "Yes," she answered. She missed her sister who was two years younger. Maybe she'd phone her, see what was happening on the West Coast.

"Wow. That's some uppance. Food?"

She nodded and he left her to her beer, squeezing her toes as he returned to his post. By the time her glass was empty, a ginormous plate of sinful nachos was set down along with a new beer. "Bastard," she muttered as she plucked a bacon bit free.

Despite agreeing to the food, she wasn't that hungry. She listened to the conversations, to the boos and cheers thrown at a game whose outcome was twenty years old. "What a sad, pretty girl."

She opened her eyes as Shayne slid into her booth. He had his own drink, a cola, and he studied her with an intense look in his eyes.

The olive green shirt made his eyes greener as it hugged all the muscley goodness that was Shayne. He took a chip loaded with cheese and peppers. Planting his elbow on the table, he offered the bite to her. "I'm not hungry."

"Don't want you passing out on me again when my hand goes down your jeans. Eat."

She dipped the chip into the small bowl of salsa and studied Shayne. "Think that's where it's going, hm?"

Instead of answering, he leaned back in his seat, his eyes smirking his answer that that's exactly where his hand was going to be later. She wondered what had brought him here. "What brings you to the Box?"

He took another sip then found the right chip he wanted. A thin strand of cheese stretched to the plate before he broke it with a swipe of his finger. He scooped a large amount of salsa and guacamole onto the chip then ate the entire thing. He sipped his soda and set his foot on the edge of her seat by her hip. "You."

"Followed or summoned?"

His eyebrow went up in answer. Summoned. "What did my baby brother say to have you don your superhero cape?"

"That you were a pitiful mess who was into her cups and cheese." Shayne pressed his foot against her hip and she toyed with the small cuff of his jeans. "Are you a pitiful mess?"

"Yeah," she sighed, feeling a little morose.

"Wanna go hit a few pucks?" He nodded his head at the door. "Come on." He grabbed his glass as he stood up, waiting for her to move her self-pitying ass.

With a sigh, she took her glass and followed him out into the night. Two people sat on the bench against the wall as they smoked. A goalie net that had seen better days was against one wall. A couple of hockey sticks were in an umbrella stand along with a bucket of tennis balls. There was even a goalie glove that had new years and years ago. "Hey," Shayne said, greeting the smokers, then set his drink down.

His foot tapped the bucket, spilling balls over the concrete pad. He tossed a hockey stick at her and she stepped back so it didn't smack her in the face. The sound of the wood clattering filled the space and she went to set her glass beside Shayne's. When she turned, he had the glove on and was smacking the sides of the goal in a head nod to the hockey gods. "Okay, Magerin, bring it."

She picked up the stick, using the blade to draw a ball towards her. The odds of her scoring on Shayne were as high as Carmen giving her hug right now. Her shot was pathetic and the ball rolled sadly to him.

He stood up straight and his sigh was loud as he kicked the ball back at her. "Jesus, you're a Magerin. Hit the damn ball--don't nudge it." Once again he crouched down, his body relaxed in the pose.

That was annoying. Lacey hunched down like him and looked him in the eye. "And the puck is dropped. It's Magerin versus Payne. Magerin grabs the puck and it's a break away." Shayne snorted as he grinned. "She goes left dodging Payne. Right. Left. Now it's two on the ice. Can she do it? Can she score on the great Donnelly?"

She grabbed the front of her shirt, flashed him her lacy bra then shot. "And she does it! Ladies and gentlemen, Magerin has scored on Donnelly. The crowd here is insane." She lifted a hand to her mouth and imitated a crowd roaring as Shayne looked behind him at the green tennis ball resting against the netting then at her. Even the smokers were cheering. Though she assumed it was for her bra and not her hockey prowess.

"I can't believe you..." he tossed aside his stick and began to stalk her. "You flashed me!"

She was laughing by the time he grabbed her by the waist and dragged her out of the small zone.

"Way to go, baby!" One of the smokers shouted.

She heard the other one. "Can they play again?"

Shayne pushed her against the side of the building, the bright lights spilling right past them at the patio. "I can't believe you flashed me." His hands settled on her hips as he crowded her against the wall. "Let's see that bra again."

His mouth was on hers before she could grab the bottom of her shirt. He tasted of all things sinfully delicious in the dark.

Chapter 7

"WORD ON THE floor is you scored on Hands here."

The glass paused briefly before Lacey took a sip. Shayne met her gaze, an eyebrow rising up and down while his foot rested between her thighs. One of her legs was hooked over his. He didn't bother to lower his foot when Todd dropped down beside him though he felt a little nervous. Shit, fifteen minutes ago he had not only seen Lacey's bra but his hand had been under it too while they had made out like a couple of horny teenagers.

"It's a gift." She lifted a shoulder in a lazy shrug.

Apparently word on the floor had left out the whole flashing part.

Todd picked one of the chips out, one not covered in congealed cheese. "Hear you got a pretty bra too."

This time Lacey coughed, choking on her beer. A pretty blush spread over her cheeks and she focused on her beer instead of her brother.

When Todd looked at him with narrowed eyes,

Shayne nodded. "It's a pretty bra. What can I say? Don't look at me like that, dude. She's your sister, flashing her bits all around your bar. Better warn the pool sharks."

Todd held up a hand. "Please. Sister. Bra. Let's not go there. These are nasty. New order?" He looked at Lacey, shook his head then took the nachos with him without waiting for their answer.

Shayne rested his elbow on the table. "Wanna go play again? Best of two. Come on." He leaned to the side and enjoyed the laugh that erupted from her. Returning to his original position, he ran his hand along her calf. He hated boots. They got in the way of skin. "Feel free to score on me any time, Magerin." He lifted his glass and smiled at the memory of that pretty pink bra. "Aaaaaanyyyy time."

Along his ankle he felt her hand glide up and down while her other elbow rested on the table, her hand slipping behind her hair. "Maybe I'll share my method with Adam."

He paused, playing the image. "That would truly stun me if Payne was wearing a pink lace bra and flashed me during a televised game. Truly stun me." He shuddered and wished the picture would leave his brain forever.

"So what did Todd say when you said you were sticking around."

"Cool." There had been a moment when his friend had wanted to ask a question. In the end, Todd had kept it to himself. It was why they were still friends after all this time. They didn't talk shit about feelings and stuff. He was staying, that was okay. And if tomorrow he said he had enough and was going home, Todd would nod, mutter a "Cool" then drive him to the airport.

"Talkative. No questions? No curiosity?"

"None he voiced." Thank God because what would he say? Oh, wanted to stay, hang out in your sister's bed and because she asked. *That* would go over well.

With a shrug, she smiled at the waitress who left a new order of nachos on their table. "Boys are weird. Thanks."

"No problem." The waitress grinned then winked. Apparently the word on the floor was that Lacey had flashed him then scored.

His ego was going to take a hefty kick but he dared any man to stand there and not be struck dumb by her breasts being flashed. Frowning, he decided that was a dumb idea and no one got to see her flash him but Shayne.

"We should eat those," she said without looking at the chips.

"Yup." He wasn't hungry. He had scarfed down a sandwich earlier.

"A girl needs her energy." She smiled as she helped herself to a cheesy chip.

"She does."

"On the other hand--"

He dug out his wallet and slapped a ten dollar bill on the table while she retrieved her purse. They went out the back where a couple of guys were having a game.

"Whoo, Lacey, gonna flash?"

Damned if she didn't turn, and start to yank up her shirt. Shayne put a restraining hand on her arm and she laughed. "Sorry boys!" She lifted her hand and waved.

"Maybe another time."

"Count on it!"

Jesus. The woman was a hazard. He snagged his hand in her back pocket and pulled her away from the parking lot. "Let's walk. God knows who you'd flash in your car."

She was clearly a little buzzed as she faced him and yanked up her shirt again. "Just you, baby." Lacey spun and laughed, almost knocking him with her purse.

He yanked her back and wrapped his arm around her waist. "You are a danger to society."

"Why are we walking? I have a car."

"You are drunk."

"No. Not drunk. Just feeling no pain. You could drive."

She would feel pain if he tripped and dropped her on her head. "You'd flash me then I'd crash your car. How pissed would my agent be then?"

"True, too true. Damn agents," she snarled the word and he almost tripped over her when she suddenly stopped. "Fucking agents. Jerks. She wasn't the first, you know." Her voice was soft and he tightened his arm on her, holding her closer.

He had assumed so.

"He stopped touching me when Carmen was ten. He left me long before I kicked him out. And it's my fault. Mine."

Shit. "Lace." He turned her and held her because there was nothing else he could do, nothing he could say. "Who said that?"

"Him."

"He's shit."

"Carmen. Kayla would say it too if she were here. If I

had loved him more. Maybe they're right because I didn't love him anymore. I stopped loving him a long time ago. Love is like a plant. It dies when it's neglected." She rested her head on his chest. "Can we not go home? I don't want to go back there yet. Whisk me away somewhere else, Shayne."

He kissed the top of her head then slid her purse off her shoulder. "Yeah, but you better not flash me on the highway."

She sighed as he felt her fingers curl on the waist of his jeans. "You're no fun, Shayne. No fun at all."

He took her to the grain elevator two kilometres outside of town. He used to come out here to escape his life. When he was younger, he'd scream as the trains went by as if the rail cars could obliterate the latest beating, the latest gossip spew of what his drunk of a dad had done. The name Granville was faded and there was graffiti decorating it.

He silenced the car and darkness dropped on them like a slap shot. Folding his arms on the steering wheel, he stared at the black, hulking building.

He could tell her he never liked Kevin, had found him a selfish prick even when Shayne had been a kid. He had looked at Kevin Hodges and had seen his dad. Only sober. A user who sucked the life out of those closest to him. Instead he reached over and opened the door, stepping out into the night. A few minutes later the other car door opened and banged shut behind Lacey. Hiking himself up on the hood, Shayne slid back, the engine heat soaking through his jeans as he leaned back to look at the stars.

She stood between his legs and he shifted to make more room for her. The car dipped and the hood gave a little pop beneath their combined weight. She leaned back, her head resting on his chest.

"Why'd you stay with him?" He watched those five words rise up to night sky as he wrapped a wavy strand of hair around his finger. How, he wondered, had Kevin not touched her? Shayne couldn't stop touching her.

"The girls," she answered in a soft voice. "And pride. Pride," she repeated with a whisper. "I kicked him out because it was no longer just our unspoken secret. It was out there in the world because lollipop couldn't keep her mouth shut that she was balling Kevin Hodges right under his wife's nose.

"He was no longer just hurting me, he was hurting our daughters. So I kicked him out. Not that they got mad at him for cheating. Oh no, that would be too easy. Poor Kevin, kicked out by their mom. What a bitch she was. Is."

"Baby," he whispered, shutting his eyes at the pain in her words. His thumb caressed her cheek and he hated the tear that he encountered.

"I wonder if Kayla would've gone to school here if I had just shut up and let him stay. But...I couldn't, Shayne. I couldn't not matter anymore. I hate him. I really hate him for what he did."

Shayne's thumb brushed along her cheek, chasing and erasing tears. She wiped her eyes then captured his hand, holding it against her chest. A year ago when Todd had called him raging about the motherfucker who had hurt his sister, he had wanted Shayne to help kick his ass. Shayne had been on board because you didn't hurt Todd's sister. Tonight he wanted to beat the man to bloody paste on the road because she was more than just Todd's sister now.

He flattened his hand over her poor, battered heart and counted stars because there was absolutely nothing he could say. Sometimes the phrase "I'm sorry" was a lame ass phrase that said less than no words. A little sigh came from her as she tilted her head into the bend of his elbow, her fingers spread over his forearm.

"Why did you kiss me Saturday night?"

Ahh...now there was a question to ask the stars. Because she had suddenly become the most tempting, amazing woman he had ever laid eyes. Because his entire body had surged alive panting like a dog in heat.

"Because I couldn't not," he answered, borrowing her words. He felt her lips repeat the words soundlessly against his skin. "Falling star," he said, pointing up. "Wish."

"I think it's a satellite," she said.

"Nah, are you nuts? That's just the longest falling star, ever." Shayne felt her smile and grinned. How to feel triumphant: make a sad girl smile. And he had done it twice tonight.

Go team Donnelly.

There was something soothing in listening to another person's heartbeat. The rhythmic pulses that meant one wasn't alone in this moment. That there was another person holding you close when your moment wasn't the happiest.

Lacey listened to Shayne's soft breathing as they gazed up at the Saskatchewan night sky. "Did you blame your mom for leaving your dad?"

"No," he said after a few minutes of contemplative silence. "I blamed her for leaving me behind. I can understand her wanting to get as far away from Jerry as she could. He was a drunk bully who hit whatever he wanted when he was drunk and angry. What did I do though? Aside from being born. I guess that was equally bad in her eyes."

She reached up to cup his face. He turned and kissed her palm. "Silly woman."

"Though if she had taken me with her, would I be playing hockey to this extent? It was an escape from the house. A way to flip the old drunk the middle finger when I made it. And if I weren't here, whom would you have flashed tonight? It is what it is, Lace. Nothing more, nothing less. And, shit, maybe she'd be worse than him. Our roads are what they are. What ifs are nothing more than insanity pills."

She liked that. "Very pragmatic, Donnelly."

"Hey, I'm not just a hot piece of ass."

He was actually the last person she'd thought to be sitting under the stars with. The last one she expected to make her feel not so shitty. And yet here he was, lying beneath her doing just that. He gave her no platitudes, offered no words of wisdom, he simply was and that was enough.

She shifted so she was facing him and his gaze shifted from the stars to her face. "Thank you."

"For what?" He brushed her hair aside then stroked his thumb down her jaw.

"Tonight. I didn't expect to get all morose about Kevin."

He shrugged as his other hand rested on the small of her back. She felt his hand grip the denim then drag her up so her position wasn't so awkward, bringing her face closer to his. "Hell, any conversations about Kevin make me morose."

"Thank you."

"Shut up." Shayne glared at her and she lowered her head to his shoulder. His hands slid down her back, over her ass and along her thighs. At her knees he gave another tug so she was straddling his waist. "Better."

Lacey could stay like this all night. Listening to Shayne's heart beating, his body warming hers and his hands holding her steady. "You're so unexpected."

She felt him kiss the top of her head while his fingers spread and gripped her thighs. "You too, Lacey. You too."

"Let's stay here forever. It's peaceful and quiet."

"Until the train goes by. You'll change your mind when it's speeding by you and your insides vibrate."

Lacey grinned. Sounded a lot like him.

"Lace?" His voice rose at her name and he cleared his throat and she smiled. "I have to tell Todd. About us."

She blinked five times then rose up to see his face. Her heart was thumping nervously in her chest at three little words. "Okay," she said, not sure how she felt about this.

"He's not stupid. And you're not a dirty little secret. Neither am I. I'd rather tell him," he sighed and looked up at the sky. "Secrets are hard to keep in Granville, especially when it's a Donnelly and a Magerin. I figure with the whole flashing and me sticking around, he's gonna be thinking something."

She nodded. "Okay. He's gonna kick you out."

"Probably. There are hotels. Unless--" An eyebrow arched up as he glanced at her.

"Yeah, because that wouldn't send my teenage daughter through the roof at all. If things were better with the girls," she lifted a shoulder in a shrug, "but it's not. It's really not better with the girls at all. You're sure about this?" Jesus, her brother. She didn't want to ruin their friendship.

Shayne looked back up at the sky. "Fuck no, I'm not sure at all."

"Okay." She lay back down on him and worried about what kind of shit was going to rain down on Shayne tomorrow. She didn't want him hurt. She didn't want her brother hurt. Hell, she didn't want to get hurt. At the end of this though, she could see them all being hurt.

WAS THERE ANYTHING more perfect than pristine ice? Shayne stepped onto the ice and couldn't hold back the grin. Beneath the sharp blade was the satisfying slice of metal carving into frozen water. It had been a slight procrastination to suggest the rink to Todd. The wisest place to have a conversation about Lacey probably wasn't on ice with sharp objects and hard pucks, but he couldn't really figure out the right place to confess.

There probably wasn't.

Why hadn't Lacey simply said that telling Todd was a dumb decision then distract him with sex? Fat lot of good she was. What was the point of being smokin' hot if you're not telling someone when they were being ridiculously stupid? He was having a word with her later on.

Pushing off with his right foot, he skated to the end of the rink. He spun easily then skated backwards as he tried to figure out what he was going to say to Todd. Clasping his hands on top of his head, he studied the empty seats that were behind the goal but found no answers.

Some conversations a guy didn't want to have with his best friend.

Sex and best friend's oldest sister was right at the top of the list. When he reached the player's bench, he slowed to a stop then stepped in to retrieve his gear. Since it was only him and Todd, he had his stick, his goal pads, mask and gloves. He strapped the pads on over his jeans. Always comfy, he thought, a wry grin escaping. All Todd needed was a stick. Jerk.

Once, younger and a lot stupider, he and Todd had done a one-on-one game with Shayne deciding to just use his gloves. When he woke up from the shot to his head, Coach had looked at him with a stern expression, "Helmet next time, boys" had been his sage advice.

A guy only needed his bell rung once to figure that was the best advice.

Hooking his helmet on the end of his stick, he carried the gloves over to the goal. Todd set the bucket of pucks on the ice then knocked it over with a loud clang. His grin was a faint reminder of the kids they had once been. With his hockey stick, Todd struck the bucket and watched it slide and spin across the ice until it hit the boards.

"There's something about an empty rink," Todd called, "that makes you want to make a shitload of noise."

Shayne nodded as he strapped on the helmet then slid the blocker on his stick hand, adjusting it to his liking. There was a soothing ritual in putting on the gloves for him. All the rest of the gear was just that. The gloves made him feel like a goalie. Next he eased on the catch glove, grinning as he folded the ends.

Oh yeah, now the game was on.

Before suggesting the game to Todd, Shayne had gone for a run then headed over to the Granville gym for a yoga class. Had to keep himself bendy and flexible somehow and if checking out equally bendy and flexible girls in tight clothes was his punishment, then so be it. He needed to get some weight time in too.

Todd was organizing the pucks how he liked while Shayne did a few stretches. It would really suck to pull a groin muscle. Talk about hindering his time with Lacey.

And now he was full circle in what to say to Todd.

Muttering under his breath about dumb ideas, he smacked the catch glove on the ice. There was a nice echo from leather meeting ice and he had to agree with Todd about the noise in an empty rink. The slap was a signal developed over a lifetime of the two of them facing each other. Shayne credited all those hours with Todd for his skill in the net. Yes, he had learned a lot at MHS, but it had been hundreds of slap shots, snap shots, wrist shots, back hand shots, shots off the bar, and practiced break-aways that had gotten him to where he was.

Todd's feet eased apart as he hunched down. He tapped the wooden blade on the right side of the puck then the left then back again. "It's Magerin facing off against his childhood nemesis, Payne," he said in an al-most identical wording of his sister last night. "Who will get the puck? In a shocking move, it's Magerin." He flicked the puck behind him and skated as if he was be-ing chased by the hounds of hell. "Oh and he's slammed into the boards." He tossed himself into the boards and spun around to grab the puck.

He hoped Todd didn't flash him. Some memories he didn't need as he watched the puck. The bastard took it around the back of the net, all the while providing commentary. What was with Magerins who needed to talk during hockey? Todd spun around and tried to get the puck past him, but Shayne was already there. At least Todd didn't flash him. He had no desire to see his friend's hairy chest.

"Moving slow there, Magerin." Shayne tossed the puck at his friend. "Skating like your eighty year old dad."

"Seventy-ish," Todd said as he pointed a finger, "and don't you forget it. Or I'll tell." He skated, dropped the puck then hammered it with his stick. He swore when Shayne dropped down, the catcher doing its job. "What do I have to do? Flash you?" Todd glared as he skated back to his collection of pucks.

"You can try." Somehow he didn't think it would be as effective as Lacey. And wasn't this the perfect opportunity to bring up the reason why they were here and Todd was armed with a healthy collection of pucks to hit at his body.

Brilliant planning.

Shayne tossed the puck in the glove, contemplating this quicksand he had landed himself in. What the hell did he do? What the hell could he say? Shit. He was fucked either way.

Dumping the puck to the ice, he gave himself one more shot from Todd to figure out his words.

"Private party?"

His gaze flicked to the visiting players' bench and the

blond asshole standing there. He shifted his attention to Todd who decided to not shoot one puck but three.

Dick.

Shayne got one, one missed the net completely, and one whooshed by him and hit the netting. "One out of five. That's twenty percent Magerin, you suck." Todd had the taped knob on the ice and looked a little GQ as he stared at Payne.

"Oooh, is he gonna bring the pain, Shayne?"

Adam stood, his own stick resting over his shoulders with his wrists dangling casually over the shaft. Damn, Shayne wanted to punch him in the nose. No reason, just pure satisfaction in seeing him bleed. Their fellow classmate stepped onto the ice as if he expected to hear a processional march or something.

"Let's go, cripple." Adam Payne slid to a stop in front of a puck, sending a spray of ice up. He slammed his stick down and looked at Todd.

"Right on." Todd took up position in front of Adam.

Fuck, Shayne thought as he rolled his right shoulder. He wished he was in full gear because no doubt about it, this was going to goddamn hurt.

The battered, rusty pick-up truck parked in front of her house was a familiar sight. Garth Luvitt had been Carmen's friend for years. Now, though, he was newly turned sixteen with a piece of shit truck that had elevated his status from computer dork to kid with wheels. She liked Garth. His shiny new driver's license was another thing.

Retrieving two of the grocery bags, Lacey walked into her house and eyed the empty living room. It was the usual place the two teenagers were found, a bowl of microwave popcorn between them as they watched a movie or fired up the XBox. The backyard was empty and that left them one other place to go. Shit. Slowly, she walked down the hall, her gaze locked on that closed door to Carmen's room.

Silent prayers filled her head. *Please don't let them be naked. Please don't let me be a grandmother in nine months. Please don't make me kill my child.*

The silence was nerve wracking. Exhaling, she stared at the doorknob. If she was Coach, she'd throw open the door. If Lacey were her own mother, no way in hell would that door be closed. As it was she was Lacey, the mom of perpetually messing up with her youngest.

Exhaling slowly, Lacey leaned against the doorframe, raised her hand and knocked. Loudly. "I'm going to have to ask if you're naked to get dressed." *Jesus, God, please don't let anyone be naked on the other side of the door.* Frantic whispering and movement came from inside Carmen's room. Fuck. Lacey closed her eyes. "And Garth, I'm going to have to ask you to leave."

So she could kill her child and find the right porch to bury her under. Feeling nauseous, Lacey walked away from the panicky scrambling feeling in her chest and went to bring in the rest of the groceries. Ice cream melted whether her home life was ideal or not. *I love my daughter, I love my daughter. Thou shalt not kill unruly teenagers.* People frowned on that. Alibis were needed.

Garth stumbled out of her house, blushed a bright

red when he saw her. A mumbled, "Sorry, Mrs. Hodges," and he scrambled into his truck. That he called her Mrs. Hodges said how unnerved he was. One of the first things she had done after her divorce was drop Kevin's last name. Probably one more reason why her daughter was mad at her. His truck stalled--he was that freaked out. Lacey watched as he lowered his head to the steering wheel, no doubt pleading to any deity he could think of to get him the hell out of this situation. Lacey lowered the trunk of her car and carried the last four bags inside.

Her beloved baby girl was there, waiting with her fierce temper stamped on her pretty face. Lacey ignored her as she put away the ice cream, wondering why it was always in the last bag when you needed it to be in the first. God, her baby girl was having sex.

Her knees were going to give out as she reached into the closest bag. Fruit went where? She stared at the grapes then set them in the fridge. "I hope to God you used a condom." She felt brittle saying those words.

"Mo-o-om, it's not like that."

Hm. Yes.

She glanced at Carmen. Her hair was mussed and her mouth had a distinct kissy look to it with the red line surrounding her lips. "I wish I believed you, Carmen." Brown eyes narrowed even as her daughter blushed, whether in anger or embarrassment, it was hard to tell.

"If I was Kayla, you'd believe me. Dad lets me be alone with Garth all the time."

Her dad was too busy boffing his lollipop to pay attention. Lacey wisely kept that opinion to herself. "You aren't Kayla. You're Carmen." She managed to put away the rest of the vegetables without throwing anything. Points to her.

Lacey exhaled as she set the canister of coffee on the counter and studied the label.

"It's Garth, Mom. We're friends. You do know what it means to be friends with someone. Or am I not allowed to have guy friends now?"

Lacey prayed to all of Garth's deities to not kill her child. "I am not the villain in your story." Lacey faced her youngest. So young, so willful, so angry, so hurt. "Don't, in all this anger towards me, hurt people you shouldn't." Carmen opened her mouth but Lacey held up her hand. "It's a slippery path you're on when you start using your best friends as weapons, Carmen."

Carmen looked at the floor and blinked several times. "I--"

Lacey waited as her daughter gathered her thoughts. Nice that she was doing so.

"We didn't have sex, Mom. Just kissed." She scraped her finger on the counter top and swallowed. "I wasn't using him. Really."

"I'm not the one you need to convince." She wished she believed Carmen. She really did. It was because she didn't want to see her youngest grow up. She wanted her young and innocent. Unfortunately she *was* growing up. Damn it. Lacey returned to putting away groceries. At this moment it was the only control she had.

"I talked to Dad," Carmen said. "About moving in with him."

She hadn't thought there was anything her daughter could say that would make her heart bleed. She had been wrong. "And what did he say?"

"That that would be cool."

Lacey doubted that. He had his shiny new toy. A fifteen-year-old got in the way of shiny new toys. She nodded. She could see the story changing in Carmenland. That she kicked her daughter out. Lacey was, after all, the villain in her daughter's story. "Maybe you should," Lacey said slowly as she put away the dried pasta, the iced tea drink mix that Carmen liked. She listened to the soft slap of Carmen's bare feet on the floor as she walked away.

Lacey stared at the jar of salsa and contemplated hurling it at the wall. Instead she set it down then fisted her shaking hand. Slowly, she sat down and stared at the two remaining bags of groceries.

How had they gotten to this point?

They fought a lot lately. It was exhausting and hard on the heart. There were moments when she felt like Carmen was water trickling through her fingers. The tighter she clutched her fists, the faster she was losing her. Shit. God damn it.

The groceries could wait. She needed a quiet spot to lick her wounds. She walked into her room, shut the door then picked up the handset by her bed. As she dialled the familiar number, Lacey leaned against the wall and slid down.

"Hello?"

She rubbed her forehead as tears blurred her eyes. "Tell me I don't suck. Carmen wants to live with Kevin." The tears fell then. Resting her elbow on her knee. "She hates me that much, Non." Her jaw ached from clenching back the screams.

"Oh, baby, no she doesn't," her best friend said. Because that's what best friends said.

"She does. I'm letting her because I think I could hate her too and I love her, Non. I love her so much but it's not enough. So tell me I don't suck because I'm drowning, Non. I'm fucking drowning."

"I'm coming over. Give me a minute to bundle up Danny. You don't suck. You're awesome. Give me five minutes."

"Okay," Lacey said, hanging up. She folded her arm over her head, gripping the phone like it was her life preserver. She wanted to call Shayne, hear his voice. She called her brother's townhouse then hung up before it could ring. The odds of Shayne answering were slim. And what? She was going to ask her brother to talk to his best friend? Fuck. Complicated and she didn't want complicated right now. She wanted safe and simple.

The doorbell chimed eight minutes after she called Shannon. She stood up and felt old and creaky. Everything hurt as she splintered apart. She unlocked the door and saw Shannon standing there, Danny holding her hand.

"Oh, honey," Shannon said and reached out with an arm, pulling her in. The sobs came because now it was safe. Someone else was here to pick up the pieces.

"I have clothes in the car and a movie for Danny. Now tell me what happened."

"Don't cry, Auntie Lacey. I'm sorry you're sad." How could she resist that? She leaned down and hugged the boy because she needed a hug.

"Thanks, pal." She pressed her face into his neck and squeezed him tight. Shannon put the DVD on and herded Lacey into her bedroom to get the details.

Shannon Koval had been her best friend since junior high when the Lewises had moved here for Shannon's brother to attend the MHS. A nurse at the Granville Hospital, she worked night shifts while her father watched Danny.

Shannon's brother had died a year after the family had moved to Granville. It had started as a sniffle, turned into a cold, then morphed into pneumonia and before anyone could process what was going on, he had passed away. He was one of the reasons why her friend became a nurse. The Lewis family had stayed despite everything.

Then, as if life hadn't been tough enough, Shannon's mother had died of heart failure in her sleep when they had been eighteen. At twenty-three, Shannon had married her high school sweetheart only to lose him in a wreck on the highway between Granville and Regina almost ten years later, leaving her and her newborn son alone. She had thought Don's death was going to destroy Shannon. She had been so lost without him. Maybe she would've given up if not for that cute eight year old boy.

Lacey couldn't comprehend that amount of grief. All that heartbreak and her friend still laughed, smiled. Life went on.

It went on. Husbands died, husbands left, families fought.

Life went on.

Lacey sat on her bed and stared at her friend. She didn't want to rehash at the moment. Right now, she wanted to bleed. Leaning forward, she hugged her stomach. Shannon sat beside her and did what she had done when she had heard about Kevin and his lollipop. She hugged Lacey and said nothing.

What could she possibly say anyway?

It would be okay? How could this be okay? She and Carmen had stopped being okay when their familiar world had fallen apart.

LACEY, HONEY, IT'S Shayne. Why is Shayne calling you?"

Lacey rubbed her eyes as she reached for the phone. She hadn't heard it ring. Truthfully, she wasn't even sure of the time.

"Did you want anything to eat?"

Shaking her head, she lay back down and put the phone to her ear. Her entire body hurt. "Hi." She sounded like she had been crying for hours.

"What's wrong?" Clearly he could hear it too.

She reached down and drew up the quilt, she felt steadier hearing his voice, hearing his steps then a door closing. Her eyes filled once more. She heard a soft rustling.

"I think I hate my daughter."

"You love your daughter," he corrected. "So much that you hurt because she's hurting. What happened, doll?"

Lacey covered her eyes with her hand. "She hates me, Shayne. She hates me so much."

"She loves you," he said calmly. "So much that when she's hurting she knows she can take it out on you."

Shannon had said the same thing. She wasn't sure she believed that. "Is that why she wants to move in with Kevin?"

"Shit," he sighed. She could imagine him rubbing his face, which would explain the raspy sound.

Lacey felt a tear escape because it was shit. It was total shit. Why was she the villain? She wasn't the one who fucked a twenty-two year old then decided to shack up with her. She wasn't the one who had thrown away twenty years. Okay, she had thrown Kevin out. Why would she keep someone who didn't have enough respect for her to simply leave instead of fucking some girl half his age? "And I need her to go, Shayne. I'm so tired of fighting with her. I can't do this anymore," she whispered as another tear fell from under her hand. Then another.

"Oh baby." His voice was low and gentle.

She squeezed her hand as if that would stop the tears. She wanted this to be easier. It was stupid, but she wanted to go back to the time before she knew Kevin was sleeping with the older sister of Carmen's best friend. Back to the moment where it wasn't so hard and Carmen wasn't this ball of pain. Unfortunately that option meant being married to Kevin and she wasn't entirely sure she could go back to that flatline of a relationship.

"Distract me, because I need it."

"I'd phone sex you up but there's a time and place. You crying in the dark isn't the time."

"Pervert." She wiped her eyes and tucked her hand under her head.

He was silent for three heartbeats. "Well...yeah. Went to tell Todd. Didn't go so well. We went to the rink only Payne showed up. So the game of one-on-one became the two of them taking shots at me. Turned into a fierce battle. I won. Elbowed Payne in the face. So really I won twice."

She listened to him describe the game. She wiped her eyes and clung to the normalcy of his tone. "So in the end," he said, "I didn't tell Todd. Procrastination."

She wiped her hand over her eye. "I thought you were trying to make me feel better."

"How'm I doing, baby?"

"Terrible," she whispered as she curled her knees up into a fetal position.

"Shit. Listen to me, okay? I may not know great parents but I know shitty ones. You're not one. When she forgets she's hurting, she adores you, but she *is* hurting. Her world has changed. It's scary for her."

"Me too," she interrupted.

"I know, but you have some control in this. She has none. The only control she has is fighting with you."

"When did you get so smart?"

"Oprah."

A weak smile escaped as she sniffed.

"Carmen *does* love you, Lacey. Both you and she know that. Don't forget it and you'll be fine. And remember, what doesn't kill you, drives you to drink."

"Idiot. Thanks."

"Stop crying, Lacey."

"Night." She hung up, sliding the phone under pillow. Then she grabbed the edge of her quilt, dragged it up over her head and cried. Her door opened and shut. The bed shifted as Shannon eased into the bed with her.

"Come here." That was not her friend's voice.

Shayne. She rolled over and his arms wrapped around her. "Oh God, I really wanted you here."

"I'm here. I got you." She gripped the back of his shirt, pressing her face into his chest. He murmured nonsensical words about it being okay and low shushing noises as he stroked her back. He massaged the back of her neck until the tears faded. He kept up the soothing sounds and touches as exhaustion claimed her.

He had come. He hadn't needed to come over but he had. She buried her face in his neck then moved, kissing him. She looked a mess. She had no doubt about it. Red, swollen eyes, snotty nose, she didn't care. She wanted it all to stop, to fade away so she didn't feel like this.

"Lacey."

"Make me feel good. Please, Shayne. Please?" She pushed against his chest, rolling him to his back. "Tell me there's a condom in your pocket and make me feel not this terrible."

"No." He cupped her face in his hands. "Because then you'll feel stupid in the morning. I want the good feeling to stay with you all day, not be fleeting. So tonight you cry, you feel sad. You can't fuck it away, Lacey."

With a tired sigh, she lowered her head to his chest. "Will you at least take off your jeans?"

"No. Because then my intentions will go down the toilet."

His fingers brushed back and forth over her hip. Her hand fisted over his chest, clinging to his shirt. "I'm glad you came."

"Me too," he said as he kissed the crown of her head. "Me too."

The next time she woke up, it was to find Shannon standing there, staring with some confusion at Shayne in her bed. God, she couldn't get into this right now. "I have to head in for my shift," Shannon said softly. "Dad will pick up Danny at around eleven. He went bowling. Carmen's in her room. She emerged long enough for a sandwich, asked where you were, then went back to her room. Why is Shayne Donnelly in your bed, Lace?"

He was keeping her from falling apart.

Lacey eased out from under his arm and hugged her friend. "Thanks for coming over. Can we do this," she waved a hand towards Shayne, "later?"

"Oh yes, yes we can." Shannon squeezed her arm. "Bye, Shayne."

"Bye, Shannon," he said sleepily from the bed, shifting so he lay on his stomach.

Lacey followed her friend to the door. "Shayne. Shayne Donnelly is in your bed," Shannon whispered, eyebrows rising. "Keeping secrets from your best friend. Shame, shame."

Lacey shut the door and went to check on Danny. He looked like such a boy in Kayla's old bed, the bedding still pink with bright, funky flowers on it. "Eight, right?"

His grin was so like his dad's that Lacey paused for a heartbeat. She had liked Don Koval. He and Shannon had pretty much given up on the possibility of children.

Eight years of trying and then bam. Only Don had never gotten to know his little boy. What a crime against all of them. "Right. Are you feeling better, Aunt Lacey?"

"Yeah," she lied. She squeezed his toes under the blankets then went to check on Carmen. Her baby.

She lay on her stomach, her dark hair in her face, and one hand fisted on the mattress. Battling life even asleep. Smoothing aside the hair, Lacey leaned down to kiss Carmen's forehead. "I love you, kid," she whispered then left her to sleep the sleep of the emotionally exhausted. She grabbed a granola bar to eat then returned to her room, to Shayne.

Kneeling on her bed, she studied him. Did he understand how much it meant to her that he had come here while she was melting down? Who the hell was this man? Easing down to lie next to him again, she contemplated Shayne. His arm reached over and his hand gripped her waist. With a tug, he drew her against him.

He shifted, sliding over her and opened his eyes as he half covered her. A finger lightly brushed under her left eye. "Sad little mama," he said, leaned down to kiss her eye then the right one.

Sad little mama indeed. Lacey traced one bold eyebrow that was a black slash above those beautiful hazel eyes. He was all hard lines and angles. So rough around the edges. Her thumb followed the long, blunt path from his temple to his jaw then along the angle to his chin. A familiar face that was new again. Her middle finger stroked down the middle of his nose then to his cheekbone. She liked the dark scruff of whiskers against her finger.

He was nothing like Kevin. Her ex was soft, not just weight-wise but life-wise. Shayne was tough--made tough by surviving his childhood, made tough by his career. He made no apologies for who he was: Tough, sexy, a little badass when he wanted to be, sweet when she least expected it. He was driven, determined but not blind to the rest of the world.

"I am trying to behave," he said in a low voice, "what with the bevy of minors in this house. You are not helping, Magerin."

How had he become *more* than the Shayne she knew?

Her afternoon had been such shit with Carmen's declaration. Everything was still shit but it seemed manageable with him here.

She felt his fingers slide through her hair. He was very much trying to behave with keeping his hands by her head. The pillow dented from his elbows as he held himself above her. He also was succeeding in behaving because against her thigh she felt the firmness of his arousal.

She behaved because didn't rub up against him.

Still it was nice to know she affected him.

"I have to go tell Danny lights out."

"But I don't want to move," Shayne said. "I like you all soft beneath me, looking at me with dark, intense eyes as if you've never seen me before. I do like," he repeated, his voice low and raspy, making her insides give a little quiver.

And so much for behaving, she thought as he lowered his head and kissed her. It was slow and intoxicating. His lips glided over hers as if he had all the time in the world. She cupped the back of his neck, meeting the lazy, delicious explorations of his lips. A shift of his weight had him lying fully on her and settling between her legs when they parted for his body.

"I have to--"

"Not move," he finished and took advantage of her words, his tongue sweeping in.

"I thought you were behaving."

"Later."

She nodded as his tongue claimed hers in another hungry kiss. He slid up and swallowed her moan when his erection rubbed against her pussy. Lacey's legs tightened around him and a soft curse came from him before all his weight pinned her to the bed. He devoured her mouth.

He had the magical ability to set her afire fast. A touch, a kiss, and she became this hedonistic throb of want. That didn't, however, turn off her brain. She pushed on his shoulder and he rolled them so she was straddling him. Oh hell.

His hands gripped her ass as he rocked her over his erection. A wicked laugh was muffled on her neck as his mouth slid down.

Bracing her hands on either side of his head, she gazed down at him. She kissed him then rolled away from him. A soft laugh escaped at his muttered curse. She approached Kayla's room, the light still shining under the door. A soft knock and she opened the door. "Lights, bud."

"Five more minutes?"

She flashed him five fingers then closed the door. The

joys of being a surrogate aunt—she got to break the rules sometimes. Passing Carmen's door, Lacey ran her hand over the wood before heading off to find food for Shayne. Clearly he needed to put something in his mouth.

In the kitchen, she picked up the cordless handset. Leaning against the counter, she debated then dialled. There was some surprise the call went through to voicemail. "It's Lacey. Carmen mentioned living with you. You better have said yes because I have. A friend suggested she needs more control in the divorce as it affects her too. I agree. This is her choice, her decision. Don't break her heart, Kevin." She hung up with a nod then set the phone aside.

It was with some surprise to see her teenage daughter standing there. She looked younger with her hair messy and wearing pyjamas. When was the last time Carmen had been wearing pyjamas at eight o'clock? Probably when she was Danny's age. She tucked a strand of hair behind her ear.

"You meant it?"

"About you moving in with your dad? Yes." Lacey fussed with her own hair while hoping there were no visual evidence that she wasn't alone in her room. Great. Now *she* was the one sneaking a boy in.

Carmen nodded as she made herself a glass of iced tea.

"Danny's in Kayla's room. If you're still up, Mr. Lewis is coming by in a few hours to take him home. I'm going back to bed. Good night, Carm."

"Night."

It was one of their more civilized conversations.

She hoped Kevin didn't welch on letting Carmen stay with him. She hadn't lied to Shayne. She and her daughter needed a break. Maybe Carmen hadn't been lying and it was just fooling around with Garth, but there was so much anger in her daughter she could see her retaliating in an irretrievable way. If being with Kevin meant Carmen wasn't so angry, then Lacey would accept that. If Carmen not hurting so much meant being with her father, then she could go. Whatever it took to make her baby stop hurting.

Shayne lay on her bed, holding one of her cameras and was flicking through the pictures revealed on the viewfinder.

"Both minors are still awake." She unbuttoned her jeans and pushed them off. He looked up, watching her as she kicked the denim aside. There was a little click when she pulled her top off. "Did you just take my picture?"

"Me? No." He was once again looking at the camera. She was surprised his halo didn't make a little "ding" it was so shiny over his head. The bra was removed and she dug out an old Husks hockey jersey to sleep in. "Better be a twenty-three on that."

She turned, showing there was no number. The bedside lamp was turned on and she flicked off the overhead light. Another familiar click had her glaring at him. "Stop taking my picture."

"But you're so sexy wearing a jersey. Be sexier with a twenty-three on it. These are good, Lace."

She crawled across the bed as he rolled to his back. It felt natural for her to settle against him, her head resting on his shoulder as they both gazed up at the camera. They were pictures of Sunday's game. "I know." One of his hands dropped to her hip where he idly traced the bottom of the jersey, pressing the arrow key.

"I still have that one you took of me when I was twelve or thirteen and I was in the net. Hangs over my fireplace."

She liked that. "This is my favourite." She tapped the screen, trying to ignore the hand sliding under the green polyester with the thick band of yellow at the bottom. The picture was of her dad in his usual position, standing on the bench, watching the game with a fierce combination of love and battle.

"This is mine." He hit the button repeatedly, flashing through the pictures so it looked like they were watching a game on TV. It was her from minutes ago, her shirt being tossed aside while a little smile curled her lips. A smile because he was watching her. A smile because he was here. "This ass." His hand caressed over it then down her thigh. "Drives me nuts. Even in picture profile."

Reaching down, she pushed aside his wandering hand. "Behave. Or you won't have to worry about telling Todd because Carmen will bust in here and tell the world."

His sigh was woeful as he set aside her camera. "Then get that thing out of my sight." He turned off the bedside light, pitching her room into darkness. "Get into bed, Lace. You've had an emotional day."

Sliding under the sheets warmed from their heat, she felt him settle against her. The weight of him was reassuring as he slipped his arm under her head, his fingers playing through her hair.

She gripped the front of his shirt, pressing her nose against the soft fabric so she could inhale his scent. "Shayne, what if she leaves me and never comes back?"

"You're crazy," he whispered. "How could she stay away?"

Chapter 10

SHAYNE SLIPPED INTO an empty stool at the bar. He felt exhausted despite having fallen asleep in Lacey's bed with her for an hour. When he woke her house had been quiet and dark. Despite some groping and kissing, there had been no sex. Never had Shayne been more reluctant to leave a bed. He'd wanted to stay with Lacey curled against him, the warm puffs of her breath brushing over his neck. She had cried again. This afternoon her daughter had done what her ex-husband had never accomplished. Lacey was crushed, maybe even defeated.

Damn it.

He hated her tears, hated seeing her in that kind of pain.

"You look ragged."

"I feel it," Shayne said to Todd. "Scotch me." His friend's eyebrows climbed but he heeded the order, setting the glass down in front of Shayne then pulling some beers for an order.

At one in the morning, the Box was rather busy for a weekday. Shayne wished everyone would fall into a black hole and vanish into some science fiction abyss. Clasping his hands behind his head, he stared into the glass of scotch that wasn't as dark as Lacey's eyes.

He was in emotional quicksand.

He had known it the minute he had talked to her tonight and heard her crying. He hadn't even acknowledged Todd as he had left the townhouse. Every instinct had said to go to her so he had. It hadn't been about sex. It had been the instinct to protect her because she was hurting, to be there because she was crying.

"Fuck," he muttered to himself as he picked up the glass and took a long sip. He didn't really taste the alcohol.

He had stayed in this godforsaken, piece of hell, prairie city for one reason. Lacey.

He should leave. Now.

Pack up his shit and go back to Texas. Right now. No good-byes, no reasons, just leave, because this wasn't good. This was not good at all.

As he watched Lacey sleep, there had been no mistaking the fact that he was fucked. He didn't want to be emotionally invested because he would leave. He couldn't stay, she couldn't leave. "Fuck," he repeated as he drained the alcohol. He tapped the rim as he stared blankly at the collection of bottles behind the bar.

God bless his friend, he asked no questions. He just refilled the glass and went off.

Because what could Shayne possibly say? *Well, I've been getting your oldest sister naked and I'm falling for her.*

Yeah.

That would go over well.

Fuck.

He shouldn't have come back for the fundraiser. If he hadn't, this mess wouldn't exist. There'd be no taste of Lacey on his tongue, no feel of her in his hands, no awareness of her tears. He sure as hell wouldn't be feeling like this.

Shayne drank the whisky like it was the water it may as well be. Frowning, he stared at the melting ice cubes and wondered where the hell the booze went.

He approached alcohol more cautiously than his friends. When Lacey and Shannon had taken him and Todd to a pub, he hadn't been as excited as his friend. Todd saw it as a rite of passage. Shayne had seen a fist at his face. It had been Lacey who had told him he wasn't his father. How she had known, he didn't know. He still heard her say that no matter how hammered he got, he'd never swing his fist.

Damned if she hadn't been right. He had yet to get into a drunken bar brawl for fear of seeing his dad's face in the mirror. He had yet to be able to handle more than a whiff of vodka. Certain beers made his stomach curdle because he saw the empty cans and bottles in the shack. Granted he also never really tied one on unless he was with Todd or Lacey, as if they alone had the power to protect him from the past.

Lacey.

Once again he laced his fingers behind his head as he stared into his glass. There was some surprise when golden nectar of the Gods splashed down on the shrinking ice cubes.

"So does she have a name?" Todd asked. Shayne heard the crunch of a pretzel that was no doubt in the corner of his friend's mouth.

"Yes. Lacey."

There was coughing from Todd, a hacking, choking sound. At least no pretzel got into his drink. Shayne took a bracing sip because this wasn't how he wanted to tell his friend.

"Lacey?" Todd's voice rose. "*My* Lacey?"

"Yeah," Shayne admitted, meeting his friend's gaze as he downed the alcohol in a way that would've made Jerry proud. "That Lacey." And because Todd was distracted, Shayne grabbed the bottle and poured until his glass was almost full.

Todd grabbed the glass and took a healthy swallow. "Fuck."

"Yeah," Shayne said, nodding his head. "That, too." That, he decided, was worthy of the left jab that came out of nowhere, slamming into his cheek with enough force to cause him to almost fall off his stool. His face throbbed where the punch landed. He really needed to remember that Todd was left-handed. "Can I finish that?" He took the glass back and drained it then set the cold glass against his cheek. "Pour me another, will you?" He was going to get utterly shit-faced because then he wouldn't have to deal with Todd. He wouldn't have to deal with Lacey. He wouldn't have to deal with the mess of his current life.

He was going take a lesson from the Jerry Donnelly book of life – get drunk, it's all shit anyway.

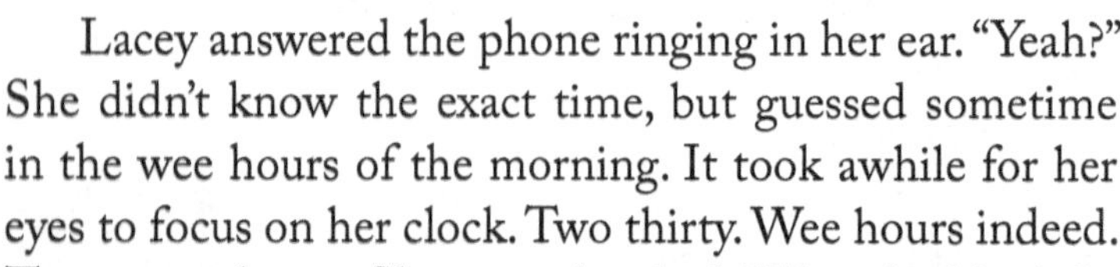

Lacey answered the phone ringing in her ear. "Yeah?" She didn't know the exact time, but guessed sometime in the wee hours of the morning. It took awhile for her eyes to focus on her clock. Two thirty. Wee hours indeed. There was also no Shayne in her bed. When had he left?

"Get your ass down here. Now."

"Todd?"

The only answer was a crash as he slammed the phone down. With a sigh, she rolled out of her warm bed and pulled on a pair of jeans. Sandals would do. As she walked by the bathroom, she stopped long enough to brush her hair. The door to Kayla's room was still closed and curious she opened it to see Danny sprawled on the bed, one leg up the wall. She knocked on Carmen's door because if there was a fire, she didn't want her daughter to leave Danny behind.

Lacey walked in as Carmen lifted her head from its face plant in the pillow. "Uncle Todd called and I have to go. Danny's still here." Not only had she slept through Shayne leaving, but the doorbell ringing too. Splendid. Wasn't she the best baby-sitter in the world? She had strange men in her room and didn't hear Shannon's dad arrive.

"Yeah. I told Mr. Lewis to leave Danny sleeping. Is that okay?"

"If the house burns down, take him with you."

"'Kay." Carmen's head fell back down.

Lacey grabbed her keys and went to see what had her brother frothing at the mouth. She squinted as she looked at the clock, to make sure the time was correct. Yep, two thirty in the morning. Yawning, she wandered out to her car then drove to the Box. The parking lot was empty but for Todd's truck so she went to the back door, knowing the front would be locked. "Todd?"

Her brother appeared like some pissed off demon. He grabbed her arm and dragged her into the bar. "Come see what you've done."

"What?" She had to jog to keep up with him. Her brother wasn't known for his temper in the family. That was solidly on Shelley's blonde little head. But that didn't mean when his powder keg went off you wanted to be standing close enough to feel the fire.

He stopped and yanked her beside him. "That's what you've done."

She stared at the denim legs bent over the side of the bench seat. She knew that faded grey shirt since it had been in her bed a few hours ago. She took a cautious step forward and saw the bruise on his cheek. "You?"

"I tend not to shake hands with guys fucking my sister."

"Oh," she said softly because what was there to say? There was blood splatter on his shirt. "You punched him in the nose?"

"No. He hit the floor. Fix that." Todd jammed two fingers. "I don't know what the fuck you did, but you fix him so when I beat the fuck out of him, he doesn't remind me of rolling his dad's drunk carcass out of my bar."

Lacey tugged on her arm then glared at her brother. Two fingers were poked towards her though he made no contact as he stormed away.

Lacey set one knee between his legs. "Shayne?"

"Told Todd," he mumbled without opening his eyes. "He took it very well."

"I see." She reached down to caress the bruise. He looked rough. Not rough around the edges but just got kicked in the head by a train rough. "Baby," she whispered because he looked so sad and broken and alone.

"Can't do this," he sighed and draped his arm over his eyes. "Fucking up friendship. Why? Fucking falling down drunk."

A painful clutch filled her heart as she began to register what was going to happen. She pulled her hand back and stared at the man who was going to break her heart. She knew it. Felt it. You always knew when someone was going to blast you apart. It was the tone in their voice. She knew it well.

"Gotta go," he said and sat up. His face drained of colour and she wondered if he was going to puke on her. "Leave. Fucking city. Hate it. Fucks with my head."

Lacey stared into the bloodshot eyes of Shayne. He squeezed his eyes shut then squinted.

"Lacey," he said as he leaned forward and rested his head against her breasts. "Sweet, sexy Lacey."

She smoothed her hand over his hair and felt him grip her hips.

"What was I doing?"

"Leaving me." She tilted his head up, kissed his mouth then walked away because she couldn't stay. Her vision blurred from tears. What had she expected? Really? She pushed open the door and stopped to see Todd firing tennis ball after tennis ball into the empty net. He stopped then straightened when he saw her.

"Lace?"

She held up her hand, stopping him because if she opened her mouth she was going to fall apart. Lacey continued around the side of the bar. The pain was a little surprising but not really. Truthfully it was leaving her feeling like she was gasping for air. She had known earlier that she was in a slippery place with him. Maybe if he hadn't white knighted it over to her place earlier it wouldn't hurt like this.

It seemed to take forever to get to her car. She dropped the keys then crouched down to retrieve them. She pressed her head against the door, her hand groping for the handle. She could do this. People broke up *all* the time. Relationships, especially doomed ones, didn't make it. And this was doomed.

So many factors were against it.

She pressed her mouth against her forearm, nodded then pushed the remote button to open the car door. The tumblers clicking open was a relief, it meant she could get in her car and leave. She opened the door and eased into the car. Slowly, painfully she lowered her head to the steering wheel and counted to five then again. Her hand was still shaking, her vision was still blurred.

A metallic bang had her lifting her head to stare at six feet, three inches of drunk male with his fists on the hood. He lifted a hand and pointed a finger at her then jerked his thumb in the international sign of "you get your ass outside."

Wiping the heel of her hand under her nose, she debated about just driving away because she didn't need to be told twice. Really.

In the end she did the only thing she could. She opened the door.

"Where are you going?"

"Home."

He gripped the door whether to keep her in or himself up. She wondered how much booze was sloshing around in him.

"No." He grabbed her arm and pulled her out. "I'm *not* leaving you." He yelled into her face.

She nodded as she pressed her fist against his chest. "Yes, you are."

"Not," he roared and thumped his hand on the roof of the car. A movement caught her attention and she saw her brother take a step forward, hockey stick at the ready. "Should," he rasped the word out. "I should."

Ah hell, he knew how to wound.

"There are hundreds of can'ts in this, Lace." He leaned down, his head resting against hers. "I can't stay, you can't leave." His sigh was pure scotch. "Can't lie to Todd. Can't wreck a friendship." He fisted her hair in his hand and lowered his nose to the strands. "Can't stay away. Can't stay with. Can't hurt you. Can't *not* hurt you." He cupped her face in her hands. "Can't, can't, can't."

Lacey uncurled her hand. "Shayne."

"Going to leave, Lace. Can't stay here. Can't be this. Can't be him, Lacey. I can't."

"You're not, Shayne. You're not."

"Not leaving you," he repeated. Neither of them voiced the *yet* that was there. "Can't," he breathed before he kissed her.

As far as drunken kisses went, it was heavy on the scotch, easy on the skill.

"Gotta go puke now," he pulled away. "Stay." He took the keys from her limp fingers then looked at Todd. "Good man, I need to barf."

She laughed and pressed her hand to her mouth as he staggered towards Todd. With a sigh, she did the only thing she could do.

She stayed.

"Here."

"Thanks." She took the glass of chocolate milk and watched nervously as Todd sat on his coffee table. They had spilled Shayne into the bed. That sounded easier than it was. Lugging around two hundred pounds of scotch and muscle was not for the faint of heart.

Her brother leaned forward, elbows on his knees as he looked at her with that gaze that gave away none of his thoughts. The sip sent sugary sweet milk coursing through her veins. Lacey focused her attention on the old graphic imprinted on the glass. She had no idea how old it was. Old enough that the fast food logo was gone. "Dad know you stole these?"

"Nope. You going to explain?"

"Nope," she said, shaking her head. How could she explain when she barely understood herself? "Carmen's moving in with Kevin."

"Fuck," Todd's shoulders drooped at the uttered word.

"Shayne called right after she told me. Told me I wasn't a shitty Mom, that I'm not a shitty person, even as he was coming to my house. He just showed up." She met her brother's gaze. "I needed him and he just..." a shoulder lifted in a shrug as confusion moved through her, "showed up."

Todd took the glass from her, probably to keep her from spilling chocolate milk on his couch. "He lit out of here like his ass was on fire. Wondered why."

"Do you hate him?" She grabbed his hand, squeezing. "You can't hate him. He *needs* you, Todd. You're his only family. If you hate him, it will destroy him." God, she had fucked up Shayne's life.

She saw the anger burn in those familiar eyes. The last time he had looked this mad, he had wanted to hunt down her ex-husband and kill him. "Please, Todd, don't hate him."

"What should I be happy about, Lacey? I just poured him into bed. Something I've never had to do before. You're crying. He's face planting. You two are fucking. What should I be happy about? Tell me!" He barked the last two words at her. He stood up and left her sitting in his living room. His door slammed and she sagged against the couch. Covering her mouth with her hand, she listened to the silence descend upon her

She should leave. Give Todd time to cool down. Give Shayne time to sober up. Give herself distance from this colossal mess.

She picked up the phone and dialled. She didn't know if she was relieved or not when she got Shannon's voicemail. "It's me. Danny's still at my place. Carmen's with him. I'm at Todd's. It's...it's such a mess, Non." She hung up and clutched the phone to her chest.

A picture she had taken long before she realized she had wanted to be a photographer was in a frame on the bookshelf filled with other pictures and a handful of books plus a huge collection of games. Even from here she could see to the two boys, arms hooked over each other's neck as they wore almost identical shit eating grins. Todd was missing a tooth. Both held up their gold medals from the provincial game they had won.

Cute little bastards.

Best friends.

Shayne had summed it up so beautiful in his drunken spewing of words. So many can'ts. And she couldn't do this to him. She was why he had a bruise on his face from his best friend. She was why he had gotten so plastered in the bar he had fallen down. She was why he was passed out. No one else. Her. How could she do this to him?

The answer was simple. "I can't," she answered the damning silence

She went into the spare room. Todd had removed his shoes but Shayne was sprawled where he had been dropped. "I'm not worth this, Shayne." She kissed the back of his head. "Ask around." He didn't even twitch.

She went to Todd's door. She flattened her hand on the door. "I'm going home, Toddy. Don't be mad at him. Not over me. Then put him in your truck, drive him to Regina and put him on a plane." She made a fist and lowered her hand because it was shaking again. "Tell him... tell him whatever but get him to leave. He was right. He can't stay here. It hurts him too much." She pressed her fingers against the wood then ran, almost taking Todd's phone with her. She dropped it in his mailbox and fled because if she didn't hesitate, she wouldn't change her mind.

If she changed her mind, she would only cause Shayne more pain and she couldn't do that to him. Last night he had white-knighted for her.

This time it was her turn.

Chapter 11

"REPEAT IT AGAIN?" Shayne stared blankly at the floor as he tried to process Todd's words. His breakfast of coffee and toast had been abandoned at his friend relaying Lacey's words. Maybe in all his hangover glory he had misheard. Everything was on strike in his body and mad at the amount of alcohol he had consumed. The message from Todd had kind of numbed all the after-effects of too much booze.

"She wants you to go," Todd said as he bounced his cell phone in his hand. "She wants me to put you in the truck, drive you to Regina and put you on a plane."

Yeah, that's what he thought Todd had said. "What did I do last night?"

"You drank. You got punched. You fell. You were dragged to a booth. I called Lacey. I left you alone. She came out crying. You went after her. You threw up. We brought you here. You passed out."

"What did I say?"

"No idea. I wasn't privy to that conversation."

Shayne looked up, meeting Todd's gaze. "Fuck, what

did I tell her, Todd?"

His friend shrugged a shoulder. "You made her cry, Shayne. You made her fucking cry."

Fuck! Shayne rubbed his chest. "I have to talk to her. Where is she?"

Todd shrugged again. "Carm called looking for her to remind her she was going shopping with a friend. I said she slept here then had some photos to go take but I would remind her."

God. What the hell had he said to her last night? He had made her cry? Jesus, he had made her cry. "Is she at Shannon's?" Another one of those annoying shrugs. Shayne rubbed his chest as he tried to recall the night from when Todd's fist had met his face. "I need your keys."

"Dude, maybe you should just...let this be."

Was he nuts? Was he out of his fucking mind? She *cried*. "I need your keys."

"Damn it, Shayne, she wants you to go."

"I don't care! Keys!" He held out his hand and glared at his friend. "I will beat them out of you, Todd. I am bigger and meaner than you. I know where to hit to make you need those pills you deny having in your cupboard." He would rip through the entire city if it meant finding her. "Keys! And your phone."

Todd drew them out and slapped them into his hand along with the phone because Shayne's cell was somewhere not in the vicinity. Apparently Todd didn't want him to waste precious time looking for it either. That suited Shayne just fine. The sooner he got on the road, the sooner Lacey could be found and the sooner this would be fixed. "This is my sister, Shayne. *My sister.*"

"I know." Shayne walked out, paused then took a step backwards. A phone was sticking out of the mailbox. "Todd! Yours." He tossed the handset over and went to the truck. He hoped somewhere along the line he remembered what the fuck he had done last night that would have her sending him away.

What had he done?

The city had changed a lot in the four years since he had been back for three days. He flung Todd's phone aside and started up the loud diesel engine. "Just one hint of what I did to her would be great. One clue. Small. I don't care. Barring that...a hint to where she is would be great." Nothing. No strike of lightning to guide him the way. No neon arrow pointing out of the spot that said, "Here's Lacey."

"Great. Appreciate the help."

He was in a city with ten thousand people. One of them was Lacey. By God if he had to talk to each and every one of them, he would.

Leave.

She wanted him to leave?

God. What the hell had he done last night? Had he ended it? Fuck. Had he? And this was why he hated drinking like he was Jerry's son and the world was going to run out of booze. "Jesus, Donnelly." He rubbed his mouth as he drove slowly down the street, squeezing his brain like the wet, useless rag that it was. For her to send him away, he must've been a real dick.

Could he plead alcohol poisoning? No. Bad idea. He grabbed Todd's phone and called his friend. "Is she at

Shannon's?"

"No. I just talked to her. She mentioned that Lacey had called last night but only to say she was here. Then she asked me what the hell was going on between you two. So I yelled at her. She hung up on me. *She hung up on me!* God damn it, Shayne. She..." Todd hung up on him and Shayne closed the phone, tossing it aside.

At a four-way stop, he folded his arms over the steering wheel and gave up on his booze amnesia. He would fix this. Whatever he had said he would fix it, if he could just find her. "Fuck it."

He turned left and decided to see if her car was at her house. Smart tactic – send the enemy scrambling and retreat to your own turf. No red four-wheel drive station wagon in the driveway. That didn't stop him from hopping out of the truck to dart around the side of her garage to peer in through the small window. Okay. Not home.

He wasn't entirely sure why he drove by the hockey rink. Hopeful thinking. It's where he'd go.

His foot eased off the gas and then he swung a u-turn in the middle of the street, ignoring the horn blasted and the middle finger salute from an oncoming driver. He drove north where the old farm used to be until Jerry had drunk it away. He had come to Shayne asking for money. It had been shortly after his contract was renewed years ago. He had been surprised Jerry hadn't come around during his rookie year but then...he hadn't earned a lot of money that year. The second year though was when the team had known what he could do and had given him some pretty American dollars to do just that.

Jerry had shown up then. There had been extreme pleasure in telling Jerry no. Then his father had gone on TV to tell the world what a selfish bastard his son was and how he didn't look after his own. Maybe he would've garnered sympathy if he hadn't been drunk and barfed on the eager, pretty journalist's shiny blue blouse. Shayne had hired the slickest, most lethal lawyers to tie up his money. Todd had been made his beneficiary in his will and after several attempts Jerry had disappeared.

Not for good. Not for five more years.

Five long years then Jerry had disappeared in the bottle of a vodka bottle forever. Glory hallelujah amen. Shayne hadn't even claimed the body when he got the call Jerry was dead.

Man, he was a bastard.

He eased off the gas when he saw the familiar car. He stopped beside it and looked at the forlorn grain elevator. Jesus, it looked like hell. Covered in spray paint, someone had also started a fire, so the front was a mass of charred wood. He walked around the decrepit building. If she was inside, he was going to kill her. This place was a fucking death trap.

He poked his head in and shouted her name. Nothing but whatever was calling this place home. He wasn't about to interrupt a rat coffee party. Or, God help him, bats.

He bent down to pick up a handful of rocks as he eyed her car. He bounced a pebble in his hand as he approached her car. And there she was. Curled up in the backseat, Granville jersey covered arm over her head. He tapped the rock against the window until her arm slid away and a tear streaked face peered up at him.

Aw, hell. She reached over and smacked her hand down on the lock. He opened the driver's side before she could move then hit the unlock button. Her hand smacked down, locking the door again. He rested one knee on the seat and draped one arm over the headrest. Placing his chin on his forearm, he studied her eyes red from crying. What the hell had he done? As he stared at her, she pushed her dark hair out of her face while new tears appeared.

"First things first: Carmen is shopping with a friend. And apparently she's worried because you didn't come home last night. And now me. How much of an asshole was I?"

"Why aren't you on a plane?"

Was that an answer? "My flight is next Thursday at two-something. If you take the first leg of the flight with me you can go see Kayla." A tear slipped down her cheek and he hated the sight of it. That one droplet clawed through him. He reached past the seat and pulled up on the lock as she wiped a hand down her cheek. Shayne stepped out long enough to open the door then crouched down. "What did I do, Lacey?"

"Nothing," she whispered, her voice thick with tears as she covered her eyes with her hand. "Nothing. Ask me what I did."

He searched her face though she hid much of it from him. Another tear though slid down her cheek and dripped off her jaw. It landed on the cream leather as loud as any gunshot. "What did you do, baby?"

"I ruined everything." She shook her head. "Like I do.

Todd's mad at you. He hit you. He's mad at me. If you go, this ends and he won't be mad at you. It will be okay."

Shayne tried to make sense of her logic. He reached out, his hand slipping under the sleeve of her jersey to stroke her wrist. "You ruined nothing. Todd will get over it."

"No," she said and pulled away from him. "If you go, this ends and then you can go back to how it should be with him. He's your family."

He tapped his thumb on the seat. "Do you want me to go?"

"Yes!" She shouted and glared at him, tears falling from her face. "Because this is hurting you. *I* am hurting you."

He nodded as he climbed into the backseat and closed the door. Shayne caught her arm and pulled her until she had no choice but to move or be moved. "Do you want me to go? Right now?"

"Yes," she whispered.

He ducked his head to meet her gaze, which she avoided, studying his shirt. "Do you want me to go?"

"Yes," she mouthed.

"Lacey." He waited until those sad, tear dripping brown eyes looked at him. "Do you. Want me. To go." She nodded slowly and he shook his. He wanted a verbal answer. "Do you..."

Her tongue darted out to catch a tear. She sniffed. "No."

He cupped her cheeks with his hands, thumbing away the tears. "Then stop putting me on a plane."

"But Todd--"

"No." He shook his head. "You and I are the only ones in this."

"But you leave--"

He didn't really want to think about that. Denial. Everyone had some. "So we got a week to figure shit out. Give me the week, Lacey. I have sixty-four--"

"Six." She gave another watery sniff. "Sixty-six."

He grinned. "I have sixty-six luscious inches left to explore. That's a lot of Lacey. A week may just do it." Fuck. He should go now. A week from now he was going to be a bigger mess. Fuck him, what about her?

What the hell were they doing to each other?

Todd had been right. He should be on a plane.

But if he only had a week left with her, he wanted that week. He *needed* that week. God help him. Jerry was right.

He was a selfish asshole.

Shayne followed her home. They had sat in her car for however long with neither of them speaking. She was tired of crying. Crying over Carmen, crying over him. She wondered if he had been thinking the same thing she was: a week from now, odds were high she'd be crying over him again as he left. Then her stomach had growled. Nothing made a moment like hunger. He had kissed her head, then swatted her on the butt.

Now he was here.

For someone who had slept a lot yesterday, she was damn tired.

"You're taking a shower," he said as he set his hands

on her hips and guided her up the stairs. He took the keys from her and unlocked the door. "I am going to feed you the breakfast of champions. Then I'm going to take you to your bed." Thumbs glided along the small of her back as he pressed his mouth against her ear. "And fuck at least ten inches of you." The words, the caress made heat shimmer through her body as he opened the door then navigated her inside.

He took her to the washroom, closed the door then removed her sandals. As he knelt on the floor, he opened her jeans and pulled them down her legs. One foot lifted then the other as he stripped off her pants then caressed up her legs. She needed to shave. Gross.

She could only imagine what her hair looked like. She refused to look in the mirror, focusing on the man instead. Through the jersey she felt his warm breath soak through to her stomach.

"What is it about a woman in a hockey jersey? So sexy to see something so feminine in something so masculine." His head rested against her stomach as his hands glided along her thighs to her hips. His fingers spread as they mapped the shape. "It stops at the teasing point, making a man wonder at the treasures beneath the shirt. God," he breathed the word out as he looked up at her. His eyes were that sexy gold colour as his fingers curled around the waist of her panties and slowly drew them down her legs. "Maybe it's just you."

"Maybe it's you," she corrected as she stepped out of the underwear and felt that slow, exploring touch up her legs again.

"No," he said, shaking his head. "I don't feel like this

when I see myself in a jersey. You though. You." His hands moved up to her waist, inching the top up to bare her pussy. "God, I wanted you last night as you undressed in front of me then pulled this on. That golden hockey stick over your breast, the puck at your belly button, the wheat blade guarding this." His mouth pressed a hot, open-mouthed kiss over her pussy and she leaned against the wall before she collapsed to the floor.

"I wanted to throw you onto your bed and bury myself in you." He caressed over her stomach, down the front of her hip then back to her waist. His lips moved against her as he talked, the words adding to the teasing touches. "Fuck you hard until you were screaming to come. Fuck that sexy wet heat of yours. Fuck you until I was spilling inside of you, as if my come could put out the fires. Fuck this pussy that calls to me, begs me even now to make the ache go away.

"Do you ache, Lacey?"

"Yes," she whispered. "I ache."

"Beautiful pussy." He parted the folds with his thumb then licked her. She cried out at the sensation of his tongue boldly tasting her, brazenly sweeping over her clit. "God this pussy that aches for me."

He reached down, drew her leg over his shoulder then licked again. She moaned his name as his tongue explored her. How could he do this to her? Instantly make her body burn for him. Or was it continuous? A continuous fire that would ease to slow simmering embers until he touched her.

"Fuck, I love how you taste. Sexy, sultry. I could live on you." His lips kissed her thigh then lightly bit. The pressure increased until it was a meaty bite that had her crying out. He traced the mark with his wicked tongue. "Look at how you cream for me." He licked the trickle on her other leg.

He was killing her. "Stop talking," she said her hips rocking forward as she tried to get him closer, where she needed him. Her foot rubbed on his back and she wished his shirt were off so she could feel his skin. "Eat me, Shayne."

"Fuck, you're hot." He smiled against her. "You're so bawdy. I love it." He stroked over the curve of her ass, drew his fingers along her pussy and made her cry out again. Back and forth his fingers stroked along her folds, to her clit then down.

The second swipe had her gasping as she arched off the wall, coming in an orgasm that ambushed her system. A little hungry sound that was almost a growl came from him and finally his mouth was on her, his tongue dipping into her as he licked up the cream spilling from her. His slick finger pressed then slid into her ass and a second orgasm took over her body.

Oh, God.

Her eyes closed as she followed the strokes of his tongue and finger working together. His other hand slid up her stomach and curled around her breast, squeezing and squeezing. She covered his hand, the thicker fabric of the graphic between them. What he did to her. "Shayne. Shayne." Her foot flattened on him as she pushed against that talented mouth.

Her body burned, an alien being that was all about need. Needed his touch, needed his skin. Needed to come.

A second finger entered her ass and her eyes snapped open as she came with a cry. His moan was muffled as he drank her down until she was nothing but a quivering mass of orgasmic bliss. She slid down the wall, settling on his lap, those fingers still pushing into her, slow thrusts that made her want more.

His mouth was slick from her. She tasted herself as he kissed her with hunger and his own need. His hand turned so he could grip the vee of her top then he slammed her to the floor, driving a grunt from her as he covered her with his mouth.

God, he can kiss, she thought as his fingers thrust deep, eased back only to bury themselves once more in her. She gripped his shoulders as she rose up into those erotic touches. She had always assumed she wouldn't like anal but then again, she hadn't counted on Shayne.

"Fuck, oh fuck, you like this." He reached down and grabbed her leg pulling her into him, opening her more. "The way you come. Fuck. Lacey."

She ground her throbbing pussy on his wrist and he swore again, his voice rasping with need. "In me, in me, in me."

"Fuck, can't leave." He fisted his free hand in her hair. "Come baby. Come for me again. And again and again."

She arched off the floor. "Please, Shayne."

"Have nothing," he growled as he buried his face in her neck. "Fuck. Fuck."

"Always have something. Bedroom. Bought them yesterday." She dragged his mouth to hers. "Coming."

"Too far."

"Yes."

"Then come again, baby. I can wait."

She opened her eyes and met his gaze. God, he was beautiful. She held his gaze as she came again, pushing against those fingers driving hard into her, rubbing that strong wrist. This time he withdrew his fingers. He lifted his hand then licked the glistening fluid clinging to his wrist before he lay down on her.

"Fucking jersey," he muttered. "Let's get this thing off of you before I have a heart attack." His grin was a little wicked as he moved to his knees then whisked her top off. "God," he whispered. "Look at you, Lacey Magerin. Look at you."

Blushing, she put her foot against his cheek and nudged him so he wasn't looking at her. He laughed then lay on her once more.

"You are the sexiest thing I have ever seen." He brushed her tangled hair off her face. "Were you always this sexy?"

She snorted. "Maybe ten years ago."

"Nah. I knew you then." He smoothed a hand down her side. "I was a walking hormone with a perpetual hard-on. I'd have noticed you."

"God, ten years ago you were in *high school*." Groaning she covered her face with her arms.

"Irrelevant." A broad hand caressed down her side, tracing the bumps of her ribs, the curve of her waist and the flair of her hip. "Four years ago I saw you and didn't have this constant urge to touch you, taste you, fuck you. So clearly you weren't sexy then either."

His hand slid to the inside of her leg and she squirmed beneath him. "Now though." His eyes flashed with heat.

"Now I fantasize all the ways I want to fuck you." He made a purring sound when his fingers glided over her slick sex and her hips rose to the touch.

Oh, god, it was the same for her. He caressed her as he stared intently at her.

"The thought of coming in you fucking haunts me." He rolled his own hips, his fingers parting the flesh that throbbed in time to her heartbeat. "How can I want you this much, Lacey? Tell me because I don't understand. I don't," he whispered the words as he lowered his head to her neck.

"I don't know either."

"Do you know why I called yesterday?"

She shook her head as he kissed her neck, traced her jaw with his tongue. "I'm glad you did though."

"Me too," he whispered as he stilled above her. "I had just showered from the game with Todd and Payne. The shower, I might add, where I jerked off because I was thinking of you." He grinned when her eyes opened. "Oh, yeah."

"Me?"

"I'm always a little randy after being on the ice." His eyebrows rose and fell. "Anyway, I was standing in that room and realized I wanted to hear your voice. Hadn't seen you yet and I wanted your voice in my ear." His damp fingers moved to her hip, back up his original path to cover her breast where her heart thudded for him. "I knew something was wrong when Shannon answered."

She swallowed; hoping the tightness in her throat would ease. Shayne lowered his head and lightly kissed over her heart. "Shayne," she whispered, incapable of saying anything more.

"I wanted to kill Carmen. I seriously wanted to strangle her for making you cry. Making you bleed." He rested his cheek over her thudding heart. "I didn't care that she's a kid, that she's *your* kid. In that one moment she was the enemy because you were crying. You scare the shit out of me, Lacey." He pressed a kiss then eased off of her. She watched him roll to his feet then lift her up. He set her in the tub then turned on the water.

"Shayne?" She grabbed his shirt and waited until he looked up at her. "It's the same for me."

His smile was sweet, causing his eyes to crinkle at the corners. He pulled on the plug for the shower. Warm water hit her in the face while the rings for the curtain jangled merrily as he sealed her in. She listened to him move around then slip out of the bathroom. Lacey flattened her hand over her heart still racing over what had just happened. "This is going to hurt," she whispered before she pushed her face under the water.

She took her time washing her hair, lathering up with cherry blossom body wash. She shaved her legs then simply stood under the water for a few minutes, replaying his words.

They were on the precipice of a nasty fall because in one week he was leaving. A part of her wished he had gotten on a plane this morning because then there would've been no bathroom floor confession. There'd be no truth that this was turning emotionally messy. She would've been able to lie to herself that it was just sex. She had lived without sex before and she could again.

Instead there was the selfish relief he was here. She

had him for a little while longer. For one more week he was hers.

A knock on the door was followed by the muffled words that breakfast was almost ready.

Breakfast of champions.

She smiled as she dipped her face into the shower to remove the stupid tears that were escaping at the thought that they were on a deadline. Lacey turned off the water and climbed out. The mirror was covered in condensation as she grabbed a towel he had set on the toilet. As she dried off, she stared at the floor, seeing him above her, feeling him inside her. Not just his touch but those words. All those words.

She hadn't known that Shayne was a poet.

She ran the towel over her head, wrapped it around her body then went to get dressed in a pair of denim cut-offs and a tank top with Houston Steam's dragon looking fierce as steam came from its flared nostrils.

She expected her breakfast of champions to be cereal. Or toast.

There was a bottle of maple syrup on the table and the scent of cinnamon clinging to the air. "You cook?"

"I have skills, baby. Mad, mad skills. Sit."

She sat and he poured her a cup of coffee. He turned and his gaze fell to the word S-T-E-A-M printed over her breasts. He set the mug down on the table and braced a hand on the back of her chair.

"I cooked for you." The words were gravelly as he brushed his thumb over her shoulder blade. "And you wear *this?*" He traced the thin strap that showed she was wearing no bra. His other hand traced where a nipple swelled through the middle dip of the M. He turned, staring at her stove, his mouth on her shoulder while his fingers lightly brushed over her. "Goddamn you."

Lacey smiled when he looked back at her. He swooped in and claimed her mouth in a hot kiss. She was distantly aware of the door banging open of Carmen's shouted, "Uncle T-"

"Excuse us. Enjoy the French toast." Shayne bent down, put his shoulder to Lacey's stomach then easily stood up.

Lacey saw the shock on her daughter's face. It faded to rage. "Shayne." She flattened her hands above his ass, pushing up. Somehow, he slid her down his arm so her feet hit the floor while keeping his arm slanted over her.

"You're fucking Shayne?"

Something hot and painful twisted in her stomach at her daughter's words. The rage hurt, yes, but not as much as the shattered look of betrayal in those brown eyes.

"How could you?" Carmen screamed even as tears began to fall. "I hate you! I'm glad I'm living with Dad. I hate you!" Her hands fisted.

Behind her Shayne went still.

"God." Carmen's gaze shifted from Lacey to Shayne then back again. "He's...you're..." Something bitter and dark twisted on her daughter's face and Lacey wanted to stop it. Stop all that pain and anger inside her daughter. She slipped away from him because her baby was hurting. "Don't!" Carmen yelled. "Don't touch me. God, he's young enough to be your kid. Gross."

Technically he wasn't. But logic wasn't the point. "Carmen." What did she say? She needed some magical spell to tell her what to say.

"No!" Carmen shrugged away from her, and squeezed past them as if she didn't want to touch either of them. "I'm going now. Now!"

Lacey flinched when the bedroom door slammed behind Carmen.

"Do you want me to go?"

No. She wiped her eye because she was damned well crying again. She nodded. "I think you should. Sorry. I'm--"

"Don't," he whispered. He leaned down and kissed her head. "Call me. I mean it, Lacey."

She nodded as she heard Carmen yelling into her phone. She listened to Shayne leave, each stepped seemed loud in her head, competing with her daughter screaming in her room. Pressing a hand to her stomach, she went to that closed door.

Normally she knocked. She doubted it would be heard. Carmen's room was a mess. Clothes trailed from the dresser to her school backpack. She picked up her daughter's favourite sweater and found herself folding it, sliding her hand over the black cotton weave. Tears were spilling down Carmen's cheeks as she tried to shove jeans into her bag already full.

Where had all this rage and pain lived in such a slender being? Carmen grabbed her bag and screamed in frustration, throwing it across the floor. "Oh, baby," Lacey whispered as her own tears fell.

"He said no. He said NO!"

Goddamn it, Kevin. Lacey smoothed her hand down the hair so like her own. She had been so stunned to see such a miniature version of herself when Carmen was born.

"Don't touch me," Carmen said, rolling her shoulder and pulling away.

"Carm." Lacey ignored her and wrapped her arms around her daughter. A painful sob ripped through Carmen and they went to their knees.

"He said there wasn't room for me. And that Amber didn't need added stress. He said I couldn't stay with him."

Her ex was a selfish ass. He was an idiot. Damn it. Lacey was an idiot too. "You can go stay with Coach and Grandma."

Carmen lifted her head, tears smearing her mascara. "You don't want me either?"

Lacey almost died at the words. "Oh, baby." She hunched over her hurting daughter. "I always want you. I love you. I will always love you."

"He's not coming home."

Lacey rested her cheek on Carmen's back as she smoothed down that beautiful wavy hair. "No, baby, he's not coming home."

"Don't send me away." She sounded five again as her hands clutched Lacey's back. "Please don't, Mom. Don't."

"I will barricade the door on you. I'll have Coach nail your windows shut. I will set dogs on you if you escape me. You are mine, Carmen Dana Hodges. *Mine.* I just want you to stop hurting."

"It hurts all the time, Mom. All the time."

Lacey gaze shifted to the door where Shayne leaned against the frame. He nodded and left them alone again.

"He will always be your dad, Carm. He's just not my husband anymore. He loves someone else."

Carmen sniffed as she rested her cheek on Lacey's thigh. "I hate her."

"Me, too." Lacey rubbed Carmen's arm.

"Why does he love her, Mom?"

"She makes him feel young and free." Lacey reached up and wiped her cheek. "He doesn't feel like he's almost forty-five years old."

"That's not love. That's a midlife crisis."

Lacey choked on a laugh then buried her face in Carmen's hair as she couldn't stop the giggles. "Oh baby. I love you."

Carmen hugged her hard and Lacey heard Shayne in the kitchen. Way to leave. She wasn't surprised he hadn't though. White knight. There when she was hurting.

"Do you still love Dad?"

Lacey shook her head. "No. We fell out of love a long time ago, honey."

"Why? How do you fall out of love?" Carmen uncurled from her protective ball but kept her head in Lacey's lap.

"Sometimes you do. You don't know why. You don't even recognize the moment when. But I will always love pieces of him. The pieces that gave me you and Kayla. Pieces that gave me the camera. It wasn't always bad, baby. We loved each other enough to make you and your sister. And we'll always love you two. You're pretty hard to fall out of love with."

Carmen looked up at her and her tongue darted out to catch a tear. "Even when I'm a bitch?"

"Especially when you're a bitch."

"I don't hate you." Her daughter rubbed her nose and tucked her hand under her cheek.

"I know. Shayne said you get angry at me because you know it's safe. That no matter what you say to me, I'll still love you and you know that."

"That's awfully smart for a hockey player."

Lacey smiled. "Yeah, he's got some brains in him behind that pretty face." She rested her cheek against Carmen's then kissed the damp skin. "Vacuum under your bed, baby, that's horrible." She smiled when a choked laugh came from Carmen. "Take a bath. Then pull on your sweats and stop worrying so much."

Carmen nodded as she sat up. She wiped a hand down her face then sighed. Slowly she stood up and headed to the door. "Mom? Do you love Shayne?"

Lacey picked up a t-shirt and began to fold it carefully. "I don't know, Carmen. I don't know." She set the shirt on her lap, her skin damp from her daughter's tears. She was not surprised when Shayne came into the room. "She doesn't hate me, Shayne."

"No." He cupped her chin and tilted her head up. He studied her face then wiped the tears away.

"You didn't go."

"No." He leaned down and kissed her gently. "French toast is ready. This can wait." He took her hand and drew her to her feet. His fingers entwined with hers as he led the way to the kitchen.

She studied the breadth of his shoulders, the sureness of his grip, and knew she had lied to her daughter. God help them all, but she did love him.

Chapter 12

SHAYNE LOOKED UP from scrubbing the frying pan when Carmen walked into kitchen. God, she looked like her mom. Breakfast had been an uneasy truce, with Carmen looking young and uncertain. Lacey had set her empty coffee mug down and had glared at him. Why he got the glare was anyone's business. She had then announced she was calling Kevin.

Carmen's eyes had gotten wider and wider the more Lacey had yelled into the phone, cursing out Kevin.

Shayne wondered if he'd get to go punch him unconscious when she was done. He very much wanted to hit the man.

"Mom is really mad."

"Yeah, she's really mad." He couldn't blame her. He was mad at what Kevin had done and Carmen wasn't his kid. The mama bear was unleashed and clawing into the body of the man who had dared hurt her cub. Didn't matter that it was papa bear either. Shayne stared at the pan then looked at Carmen. "Look, I know this is weird for you."

Brown eyes rolled at his understatement. She screwed the cap back on the syrup and put it away. God, she was like her mom. So full of sass. "It's weird for me too, Carmen. Weird for Lace. Weird for Todd. It's just...weird."

He rinsed the pan off then set it in the drying rack. "Did you know what I was doing one week ago?" Folding the cloth, he then leaned against the counter as she put away the rest of the ingredients. When she flicked a look at him, he continued on. "Unpacking. No way was I getting on that plane. Five minutes later I was packing. Fifteen minutes after that I was trying to figure out how to cancel my flight. Then came Friday and damned if I was in the goddamn taxi going to the airport. I kept hoping I forgot my passport so I couldn't get on the plane."

"Well I don't give a shit!" Lacey yelled from her room.

He grinned and mentally high fived her. *Go, baby.* "Unfortunately I had the goddamn passport and I was getting on the plane. Hoped it would crash. Boom. No more having to come here. It landed in Calgary. No problem." He glared at that. "I didn't miss my flight. It was fucking on time. Got off the plane and there was your bloody uncle. I hate this place," he sighed, rubbing the back of his neck.

"Why?"

"It's got a lot of shitty memories for me. Then came Saturday. Jesus." He rubbed his mouth as he lost focus. "She was this goddess. Beautiful. Most beautiful thing I ever saw." Carmen hopped onto the counter, watching him. "I was reeling and then she smiled at me and it wasn't a shitty memory.

"So this is weird for me, Carm. Really fucking weird."

"Well, fuck you too!"

He smiled as he looked over his shoulder. Her door banged open and he listened to her stomp down the hallway. "Two minutes for bad sportsmanlike conduct, Magerin." She lifted her hand and flipped him the middle finger. He grabbed her wrist and drew her into him. "You okay?"

"Go hit him. Just...hit him."

"Really?" His mood perked up. He rubbed his thumb over her wrist. "Can I borrow your car? Todd's truck is gone."

She sighed and rested her head on his chest. She shook her head negatively. Damn it. He wanted to hit the bastard.

"Get your skates," he said as he kissed her head. "Both of you." He took the phone from her and dialled Todd. Carmen was studying him, her head tilted to the side. She looked a lot like Coach in the way she was mentally dissecting him. "Rally the troops" he said once he heard Todd's voice on the line. "Game's on. Bring my shit to the rink. Thanks." Hanging up the phone with a flourish, he ran the back of his fingers up and down Lacey's arms. "Let's see if you can score without dirty tactics, Magerin."

"Blow me."

He lowered his head, his mouth against her ear. "Not in front of minors. Put on some pants." He watched as Carmen hopped down from her perch and darted from the room. God love the Magerins. They were so easily distracted with hockey.

Lacey smiled as she listened to Carmen and Todd argue in the kitchen about how her penalty was unfair and he had purposefully tripped over her stick because he was losing. The game had been fun. In typical fashion they had all swarmed on her parents' house where dinner had consisted of pizza and popsicles.

"You awake there, Magerin?"

"Basking in my win." Plus the sofa was surprisingly comfortable. Would her parents miss it if she dragged it home with her one day? In the family room, the television was on and she could hear her mother discussing some luncheon thing with Janine. The last she had seen Coach, he had wandered into the kitchen, no doubt to watch his son and granddaughter bicker. He always knew how to find a good game to watch.

"You horrified your brother-in-law when you flashed him. Tsk."

She grinned without opening her eyes. Shayne sank down beside her and caressed down her arm. Her skin prickled beneath his touch. "It worked."

"Don't do it again."

She opened her eyes as he leaned down and kissed her slowly. "It wasn't like it was my bra."

"This is killing me." His hand glided over her stomach, petting the dragon decal. "Come for a walk with me." His hand tugged up the fabric of her top. Her breath caught as his fingers brushed over her stomach. "Come get naked with me." He lowered his head and kissed her stomach, his tongue circling her belly button as he tugged on the tie of her yoga pants she had worn for the game. The man was stripping her in the middle of her parents' living room with family scattered *everywhere.* "Every time you bent down in these pants..."

His hand glided over her hip, following a mental path in his head to her ass. "Shayne," she whispered as his hand tugged on the back of her pants. She gripped the front because of that bit about family being everywhere.

"You smell of hockey." He licked up her stomach as he covered her, sealing his mouth over hers.

Holy hell. His tongue conquered hers as he rocked his erection against her while pulling on her pants. Maybe they should have gone back to her house. Shayne's mutter of, "This is a bad idea," suddenly made a lot of sense.

Ice did indeed make him randy.

"Let's go," he whispered, tugging at her shirt and pulling at her pants. "Get naked. Tired of not being inside you." He slowly pushed his pelvis into hers. "Want to come inside this hot, hot body." His mouth closed over hers as his hand slid beneath her pants. "Want to pound into this hot, steamy pussy. Fuck you now."

He stroked her pussy as he pushed up her tank top and lowered his mouth to her breast. "Come with me, baby. Come with me."

Holy hell. She nodded and he gave one last slow, caress over her damp sex then he was up. He dragged her to her feet while she pulled up her pants. His walk consisted of going up the stairs to the spare room and shutting the door.

He pinned her against it as he kissed her hungrily.

His hands pushed at her pants then palmed her ass with one hand. "You smell of ice and sweat and pizza." He lowered his face to her neck as he inhaled. "Fucking in you *now*."

He spun her away from the door and dropped her onto the bed, wrenching the pants down and away. A hiss escaped him as he leaned down and licked her pussy, making her arch on the bed. Her hands gripped the top. "Leave it. Fucking leave it on." He flipped her onto her stomach and settled his weight on her. He rocked his cock against her ass as he bit her shoulder.

Holy hell.

Her hands fisted on the bedspread, the bed muffling her moan as two hundred pounds of hard, aroused male rubbed against her. What was he like after a playoff game?

The thought made moisture spill from her pussy.

"Want to come in you," he whispered in her ear as he caressed her hips, her thighs. "God you smell so goddamn good, Lacey."

He smelled pretty damn good himself. A little sweatier from wearing his pads, with a tinge of leather blending in. "Oh God, Shayne." She pressed her face into the bed as he rubbed against her ass. He eased off long enough to open his jeans and then with a low, hungry growl he was thrusting into her. She cried out as he filled her.

"Oh fuck, yes." He lifted her hips, then began to do exactly what he said he was going to do. He pounded hard into her, his fingers bruising her hips. He felt huge as he pumped hard into her. Thumbs rubbed back and forth over her ass. She wished she could see him like this.

She could only hold onto the bed as her orgasm crashed violently through her. A savage sound came from him as he slammed one final time into her and shuddered as he came.

They collapsed onto the bed and he eased out, rolling her onto her back so he could kiss her. He stood up, yanked his shirt off and flung it aside. He battled his jeans and underwear, paused long enough to tug off the condom he had put on, then he was on her again.

"I love this," he growled as his fingers dragged over the letters on her chest. "Love it." He lowered his head and bit her nipple through her top. "Love me on your tits." He rested his chin on her breast and looked at her, his eyes gleaming with arousal. "Going to fuck your tits. Then I'm going to come in your mouth." He traced her mouth that parted at his words. "Two inches. Then I'm going to fuck your ass again because it drives me crazy. Then after I fill that luscious ass with my come, I'm going to take this pretty pussy and make it mine."

She blinked. "Okay." She dragged him up and kissed him, swallowing his laugh, his moan and then he did exactly what he promised to do.

God, she loved hockey.

Lacey looked up as Shannon sat beside her. Her friend looked tired. And sad. "What's wrong?"

Shannon shook her head. Danny was on the ice looking starry eyed as Shayne was showing him how to hold his balance in the goal. "Shayne Donnelly?"

Lacey nodded. "Shayne Donnelly." The night after

the hockey game, he had stayed at her house. His goalie equipment was spread out in her garage. Her daughter even seemed okay with his being there. Her life had become severely weird.

And she was running out of time.

Thursday, inevitable fucking Thursday, was racing towards her like a slap shot and she wasn't sure she was going to survive. Shannon had called, a little embarrassed to ask if Shayne would spend some time with Danny on the ice. Lacey lifted her camera and zoomed in as Danny was shown how to hold the goalie stick. Somehow word had gotten out that Shayne Donnelly was on the ice and he was gathering a crowd.

Whatever he was telling Danny, the kid was paying close attention. Lacey looked at Shannon then rubbed her arm. "You look..." she searched for the right word. She hadn't seen her friend this sad since Don had died. It was a little scary. "You look lost, Non. What's going on?'

Shannon lowered her head to Lacey's shoulder. "I messed up. I *fucked* up and it's a mess. It hurts."

"You can tell me, Non."

"No, Lace, you're the last person I can tell."

Lacey hugged her, worried at what had happened. "When you're ready to tell me, you know where I am." She rested her cheek on Shannon's head and watched as Shayne half slid to the bucket of tennis balls. No skates for this lesson apparently. Even Danny wasn't wearing them. "I'm in love with him," Lacey admitted, her vision blurring briefly as Shayne began to roll balls at Danny. The wide blade of his goal stick slid to his foot then the middle then the other foot. Learning the weight of the stick. Her dad had done that with Shayne. Danny's other arm was sticking out to the side to help hold his balance. God, they were cute.

"Shit," Shannon whispered and lifted her head. "Lacey…"

"And in two days he's leaving. It hurts to know in two days he's leaving." Thursday at two-something. She swallowed and watched him straighten and look at her. She bit her lips to keep them from quivering even as she lifted her camera and caught his picture. Did he know she was sitting on this cold bench, her heart aching because in forty-eight hours he was gone?

"What's going to happen?" Now Shannon was hugging her, a familiar arm wrapped around her.

"He goes to Houston. I stay in Granville. Nothing," she whispered as she looked up at the lights. "Nothing. God, look at him. He's thirty in November, Non. *Thirty.* I've known him since he was four and…" she swallowed as she wiped her eyes. "And he's got so much of my heart it scares me. How did this happen?"

"Does his age matter?"

"No. Sometimes he seems older than me." She fidgeted with her camera, needing to do something with her hands. "He and Carm sit in the backyard and have these long talks. He understands her so much. All that pain from the divorce. He gets it because his mom left and he knows all about raging pain from his dad. He doesn't tell me what they talk about it. Private, he says. When he goes," she watched him bounce a ball on the ice as he continued his lesson with Danny, "he's going to break my daughter's heart."

"Her mom's too."

"Yeah." Across the ice, she saw Todd watching, his arms folded on the boards. It was still not good between them. Had the family game helped? Only until they had gotten off the ice. "I broke them," she whispered.

Shayne bounced the ball again and she half expected him to turn and heave it at Todd. He didn't. His attention was on the lesson.

"Who?"

She nodded her chin at her brother. "He's so mad at Shayne. God, he's mad. I don't know if Shayne coming to my place made things better or worse."

"Todd's tough."

Lacey knew that for the lie it was. Todd looked at them and Lacey lifted her hand to her ear, mimicking a phone then pointed at Shayne. Her brother pushed away from his slouch and she watched him walk around the boards. He stopped behind the goal and knocked on the Plexiglas. When Shayne looked up, Todd lifted his left elbow then continued. Shayne bounced the ball then said something to Danny. His elbow lifted and Lacey felt something like relief mow through her.

Todd nodded at her as he slipped out the door. Okay. She sighed. "Okay," she whispered. Maybe they weren't as broken as she thought. "I'm going to be right back." She handed over her camera and scampered down the bleachers and chased her brother.

"Todd!"

He paused at his truck, digging out his keys. She jogged towards him and hugged him.

"What was that for?"

"You needed one," she answered as an arm wrapped around her. Oh God, he looked lost. She had hurt her brother. "Come to dinner tonight."

"What?"

"You. Come over for dinner. This is stupid. He's your best friend."

Todd rested his head against hers as he tugged on her hair. "And you're my best sister who in a few days is going to be crying because he's gone."

And she would have everyone's shoulders to cry on while Shayne's had no one. "He needs you, Toddy." She kissed his cheek. "Five o'clock. The only answer is yes." She hugged him harder because he was her best brother who was hurting now. "Five," she repeated then let him escape. She returned to the rink and Shayne looked up as she walked in.

She smiled at him because to not smile at him was impossible. She climbed the bench seats until she reached Shannon who was leaning forward, her elbow on her knee and her chin in her palm. "You should come over for supper tonight."

"What?"

"You and Danny. I think you have a goalie, baby."

"He looks good, doesn't he?" She smiled as she watched her son. "Are you matchmaking with my son, Lacey?"

Lacey grinned as she leaned forward resting her elbows on her knees. "Me? Would I do that?"

"You're a Magerin," Shannon snorted. "Fuck, yes you would do that. Yeah we'll come. Danny, hit the lockers."

"Moooom!"

Lacey watched Shayne bounce his ball on the ice again, grinning. He flicked his wrist and tossed the ball at the bucket. It missed and bounced across the ice. Todd's words came back to her "*He can't shoot for shit.*"

"But talk to my brother about teaching Danny to shoot," Lacey said as Shannon gathered up her things. "Five?"

"We'll be there."

Lacey watched as Shayne retrieved the neon green ball. He half slid and half pushed himself to the bucket then the boards. He lifted Danny over then rested his arms on the wood and looked at her. She raised her eyebrows and let them fall.

"Bad, bad girl," he said as he handed the bucket to Danny then walked toward the main gate.

"What did I do?"

"I dunno. Let's go think of something."

She laughed as he stepped off the ice then she took the hand he held out. "You are a bad, bad man, Shayne Donnelly."

"Yes," he said as he lowered his mouth to her ear, "and I was just on the ice."

Her heart gave a little thump as his hand squeezed hers. His eyebrows rose and fell in a much more effective manner than hers. "I love hockey," she sighed as he pulled her through the entrance and out into the parking lot.

Shayne pulled her to her car. A man on a mission to get her horizontal as soon as possible. She leaned against his back. "If you make it to the playoffs, I'm going to every single game."

He jerked to halt then spun around. A hand caught

the back of her head and he kissed her while his other hand grabbed her ass and drew her into him. "Incentive. Me likey. Let's get naked, Magerin."

"Yes, Donnelly. Let's."

Chapter 13

"AW, YOU CHEATED," Carmen said as she glared at Garth. The tall skinny kid blinked innocently and focused his attention on the video game. Muttering to herself, Carmen focused on the television screen.

"Should I tell her how to win?" Shayne murmured in Lacey's ear.

"Shut up. That's my kid."

"You're right." He caressed her stomach. "She'll figure it out soon enough." He laughed at her look of horror. God, she was fun. She sat on his lap, watching the three kids on the couch. Danny was trying to tell Carmen what to do to advance. He bounced on the couch and told Carmen to shoot. Somehow dinner had become a group event and he wasn't sure he liked it.

"Door was," Todd walked in and came to a grinding halt, "open."

"Bad, bad girl," Shayne muttered in her ear as he looked at his friend.

"Hi, Uncle Todd," Carmen said without looking

away from the game.

"Hey, Carm." He stared at Shayne and Shayne wondered at the etiquette of having a friend's sister on one's lap.

Didn't he deserve a warning? He rested his chin on Lacey's shoulder, staring at her. She blushed and traced the seam on the armchair. "I'm going to check on the meat." He stood up and tossed her onto the cushion at the same time. Bracing his hand on the back of the chair he leaned over her. "What are you doing?"

"Making you two talk." Her foot pressed on his hip, gently pushing. "Take Mr. Scowly-Pants with you." Her gaze shifted to Todd.

Did she think they were going to magically fall into a hug, cry and everything would be fixed? Christ. He walked into the backyard, heading over to the barbecue. Fuck. Rubbing the back of his neck, he turned and faced Todd.

"So. Coaching toddlers now?"

Shayne folded his arms over his chest as he shrugged. "Keeps me out of trouble." Distracted him from the fact that there a countdown to departure going on in his head. "You should try it."

"Coaching or staying out of trouble?"

"Pick." He turned and lifted the grill dome, checking on the meat. "I need a ride Thursday."

"Lacey's not taking you?"

Shayne did not want a security gate good-bye. An impersonal kiss surrounded by strangers. No, he didn't want that at all. "No," he answered quietly.

"How's it going with Carm?"

"Okay," Shayne said as he lowered the cover and sank down onto one of the patio chairs. "She's handling this a lot better than her uncle."

"No shit," Todd said as he looked over his shoulder towards the house where Lacey was. "But she isn't going to be the one to pick up the pieces of my sister."

Shayne dragged his hands down his face and leaned forward. "You think this is easy, Todd?"

Todd stared at him. "Do you love her?"

"What?" Shit. Fuck. He stared at the concrete square beneath his feet. Todd repeated the question though Shayne didn't need him too. "I don't know."

"Then yeah, I think this is easy. I like my steak a little bloody." He pushed open the sliding door and stepped inside.

"Fuck." Shayne clasped his hands behind his head. Fucking Magerins. Get inside a guy's head, root around until there's nothing but goo then leave him flattened on the patio.

"No blood, I see."

He stared at the bare toes that appeared in his line of view. "Don't." She wore a denim skirt, baring a lot of leg to his muddled brain. She took a step towards him so his head pressed into her stomach and her hands glided softly from his elbows to his fingers. "You can't fix this. I know you want to but what is going on isn't fixable." He lowered his hands. His eyes closed as her fingers brushed the back of neck, over his hair. "I'm fucking his sister. I'm leaving his sister. I'm going to hurt his sister."

He caressed the back of her knees, loving the softness of her skin. "You can't fix that with barbecue and wishful thinking." He stood up and kissed her mouth. "I want them gone," he whispered as he rubbed his thumb up and down her cheek. "All of them gone because I'm running out of time with you. I'm selfish enough to want every minute with you to myself. Why are they here, Lacey?"

She wrapped her arms around his neck. "Because you won't be," she whispered.

Fuck. He lowered his face to the curve of her neck. "Get rid of them. God, Lace, just get rid of them." He stroked the small of her back and he didn't want to go inside where too many people breathed. He didn't want to hear them laugh. What the hell was there to laugh about? He didn't want to talk because he had no small talk in him.

A hand pushed on his chest and he sank down, exhausted suddenly.

She settled on his lap, her head resting on his shoulder. "There. Just us."

He caressed her bare leg. She had the softest skin anywhere. He draped his arm over her bent knees, spread his hand over the swell of her ass then lowered his face to her neck. How the hell was he going to leave her?

How was he going to sleep without her beside him?

She stroked the back of his neck. Suddenly her arm hooked over his neck and he felt a dampness on his neck. "Shit, don't," he whispered as his hand slid up her back. "Don't."

The little hiccup slashed at his insides even as her bent legs pressed into his ribs. More dampness as she cried. Fuck. His hand fisted on the back of her shirt.

God, all the lies they had told themselves were falling apart at the seams. He was leaving her. He could stay another week. Training started two weeks from Monday to work off the summer rest. Then the pre-season began a month later. Then the season would begin.

Maybe they'd get one or two visits in. Maybe. But school started soon and she'd be busy at MHS and with her own girls. How long, he wondered with panic, would they last with him flying everywhere but here and her here? His time was dictated by games and that was just the regular season. There were the playoffs.

Fuck. Fuck. Fuck.

A hand pressed against his cheek, turning him so her damp mouth found his. She tasted sad and salty.

All those can'ts were coming home to roost and becoming two inevitable truths: he was leaving, she was staying.

A tear slid over his nose as she kissed him, frantic and hurried as if this moment was about to vanish. A hand clutched his sleeve as her tongue met his, her tears blending into the kiss. He was greedy enough to take the kiss, claim it for himself.

"You need to know," she whispered in the little cocoon they made.

"No," he said interrupted her. "No, I don't." God, he didn't need to know anything. "Please, Lacey, don't." This was already hell. He drew her mouth back because if they were kissing they weren't talking. "Lacey."

"Make it last," she whispered. "Make it last."

He wished he could. God damn it. He reached down and dragged up her skirt, shifting her so she straddled his lap. She cupped his face in her hands as they kissed a little more desperately.

"Now, here, take an inch, Shayne. Take an inch."

Fuck. He leaned back and gazed up at her. With the backs of his fingers, he wiped away her tears. Whiskey eyes looked at him as she rested her hands between them, fingers plucking at his shirt. He cupped her face and drew her down. Her lips were damp from her tears and their mouths. He felt her hands unbutton his jeans and ease the zipper down. He wasn't hard.

Hard to be ready when she was crying over him. Her lips sealed over his, her tongue flicking in as her hand began to caress him. Her touch was hot as she stroked from base to tip. His cock twitched to life because a Lacey touch had conditioned it to know soon it would be fucking her.

She leaned against him as she teased the swelling head with fingers. "An inch," she whispered and his eyes opened.

So it was.

"Look at me," he ordered as he caressed down her arm. Lashes lifted as his fingers folded over hers. "Are you wet?"

Her tongue licked her lip and she shook her head. Yeah, he figured. He reached down and tugged aside the swatch of her bikini panties. "Make yourself wet, baby."

She blinked then exhaled slowly. "Shayne."

"You made me hard, now make yourself wet." He traced the line of her spine through her top. "Another inch," he whispered as he guided her hand between her legs.

He forgot that on the other side of the glass door was

her family and friends. That steaks were cooking a few feet from him. He watched as her fingers brushed over the dark curls and approached her clit. "It's not a bomb, baby."

She snorted then smiled. She leaned in and kissed him, slowly and deeply. Her tongue meeting his in slow, sensual glides while he felt her fingers begin to explore all her sexy softness. He knew when she was getting wet by the way her breathing changed. He caressed her back, letting her continue what she started.

She navigated him so the head of his cock brushed her clit. She gasped, sighed then did it again until she was rubbing him, her flesh growing damper. Sweet God. His head fell back as she drew him down to the damp entrance. Her body gave a little jerk, a shudder and cream spilled over him. He clutched her ass as he looked down to watch her tease her pussy with his dick. "Oh fuck," he moaned arching when her hips rolled forward taking him deep into that warm, damp channel.

She reached back, gripping his knee as she eased back then forward. He watched as he slipped into her, spreading her with his flesh. "Shayne."

All those tiny feminine muscles squeezed him as she pushed forward over him. Her head fell back and his gaze shifted to her face, to the quiver of her breasts with her tight nipples, then back to where she kissed him intimately. One more slow thrust over him had her entire body jerking. His fingers dug into the flesh of her ass as she clenched around him then came with a hard shudder.

"Fuck," he whispered. "Fuck."

He grabbed her ass and pinned her against him as

his own body shuddered in response. She cried out as she felt him spill into her. Fuck. His knuckle traced the damp curls then the flesh still holding him deep then he lowered her face to her breasts, his body shaking with pain.

"Shayne." She bent over him, holding him. "It's okay. It's okay."

"Lacey. Fuck. Just...fuck." In days he was going to be in his condo. There would be no Lacey. No more inches. He would be alone.

He wanted her to come with him. It was a stupid, juvenile thought, but if she loved him, she'd come with him.

Just once, he lowered his face to hide his thoughts, he wanted someone to love him enough.

Chapter 14

FIVE AM WAS a horrible time when a body slid away. Lacey refused to open her eyes to watch him leave. A knuckle ran down her spine. He pressed a kiss to her head but she would not watch him leave. There was the slid of denim, the zip of a fly. The muttered word "fuck" then him walking out of her room.

Out of her life.

She opened her eyes when she heard him heft up his hockey bag then open the door. She rolled out of bed and on her tip toes she ran into the living room. Todd's truck rumbled at the curve and she watched Shayne toss the two bags into the back box. She knew he swore again as he climbed in.

Resting her head on the glass, she flattened her hand as the truck rumbled away.

God.

Her knees buckled and she sank to the floor, watching until a neighbour's car blocked the taillights. Gone.

She wasn't ready for the ache in her chest as she bent

over her knees, flattening her hand on the floor. It hadn't hurt this much when she had realized Kevin was having affairs. It hadn't hurt this much when she made him leave. Had she even cried?

"Mom."

She felt Carmen's hand on her back as she knelt beside her. There was all this pain inside her. He was gone. She choked on the sob because she could imagine the truck would be approaching the lights now. They'd turn north. Then a left turn to the bridge. Over the tracks. In more minutes they'd pass the Box then MHS. Five minutes after that they'd take the cloverleaf turn and hit the highway where they'd go south. Two hours.

"Mom, please." Carmen's hand flattened on hers where she was mapping out the route her brother would take as Shayne left. "Please," her daughter whispered. "I don't know what to do. Mommy, I don't know what to do!"

Lacey grabbed that shaking hand because neither did she. She could only sob at the pain inside her, uncaring that she was frightening her daughter. Because he was gone.

Shayne was gone.

He had come into her life, swept her off her feet, reminded her heart it felt, reminded her body it was alive and then he left. No words, no promises because there were none.

And he didn't know she loved him because he didn't want to know.

Chapter 15

"IF HE SUCKED any harder, he'd be giving Payne a blow job."

Lacey looked away from the television she was pretending to ignore to study Todd. She paused as she looked closely at him. He looked tired around his eyes. When had she become so self-involved she hadn't noticed? She rose up, her feet braced on the lower rung of her stool and reached over the bar. He caught her hand then lowered it to the smooth wood surface. "Todd," she whispered, "what's wrong?"

He shook his head as he grabbed a pretzel from the bar, tucking into the corner of his mouth. "His preseason sucked," he said, folding his arms over his chest. He watched her as half the bar cheered and the other half booed. Someone fired a plastic dart at the television screen.

Lacey fought the urge to look. She lost.

Looking up for the replay of the puck sliding right through his legs, his glove barely making it as he tried to get the puck. God, Shayne. She could almost see him mouthing a curse under his face-mask as he smacked the ice with the glove.

"His game's for shit," Todd said as he braced a foot on the cabinet, watching the goal be played again in slow motion. His bright blue eyes shifted to Lacey. "Fix it."

She once more looked at the television. "This is my fault?" The Steam were down by three now and the second period was almost over. The first game of the regular season was not going well.

Todd knocked on the bar and she looked away as Payne faced off against a Steam player. "You have his heart. He needs it to play." Todd dropped his foot and braced his hands on the bar as he leaned forward. "Give it back."

She scrubbed her finger over a gauge in the wood, focusing on it was easier then meeting her brother's gaze. "Todd–"

"You're miserable, Lacey. You're fucking breaking my heart. Carm says you cry at night." He rapped his knuckles on the wood to catch her attention again. "*Every* night. He's so goddamn miserable he may as well be catching bowling balls." He waved at the television. "I worried so goddamn much about you hurting that I forgot about him."

She swallowed as her gaze flicked to the TV. The commentators were talking about how it was looking to be a bad season for Shayne Donnelly.

"Look at him, Lace. Look beyond the mask, beyond the padding. Fucking look *at him*. I love you. I goddamn love you but you're fucking destroying him."

She lowered her head to the bar, resting it on her arm.

"So fix this." He leaned down and kissed her head. "Do you love him?"

"Yes," she whispered as she stared at the television.

"Then, big sister of mine, what the fuck are you doing in my bar?" Todd left her as the buzzer drifted from the sound system. On TV, the camera tracked Shayne as he glided off the ice. God, she missed him.

It was this constant ache inside of her. She missed that smell of him where it was the faint cologne still clinging to his skin beneath the sweat of his run. She missed seeing him sitting beside Carmen in the backyard, his body so large and protective beside her daughter. She missed the feel of him against her as he whispered lewd images into her ear. She missed how she didn't feel so alone with him nearby.

Every day. *Every day.*

A few weeks ago she had dragged her sorry, self-pitying ass to the store where she had bought a pregnancy test. She hadn't felt pregnant or anything, but two condomless times weren't good. So after praying to the hockey gods that she didn't fuck up his life, she had peed on the stick to find she wasn't pregnant. She had cried. Part relief, part sadness that there was no little bit of Shayne left in her.

She didn't want to watch the Steam lose. Sliding off her stool, Lacey walked out of the Penalty Box and headed for her car. She leaned forward and rested her head on the steering wheel.

For some reason she was surprised that two angry fists didn't slam down on the hood, revealing a very drunk hockey player who swore he was *not* leaving her. "But you did." She slid the key into the ignition then drove home.

The light was on in the living room and she stared at the old Toyota parked in front of the house. Now what was Kayla doing here when she had school? More importantly, what was so horribly wrong her daughter hadn't called to say she was arriving?

As she walked in, she heard the hockey game back on. She set her keys beside Kayla's and kicked off her sneakers. Her daughters sat identically on the couch. Sideways, facing each other with their legs bent though their attention was on the game. "Another shot went in," Carmen said quietly.

Damn it, Shayne. Lacey sat down between the two sets of bare feet. "What's wrong?" She looked at Kayla and blinked. She didn't look like a kid anymore. Sometime this past year, her daughter had started to grow into a young woman. Her face didn't look so youthful, so like the child girl she remembered. Her bangs were longer and hung over one grey blue eye. At Christmas she'd be twenty. Her baby wasn't a baby anymore.

A gasp from Carmen had her looking at the television. Oh God. Payne had the puck and was an arrow down the ice. Stop it, she pleaded. If it went in...oh God. The puck went left, right, left then was slammed by Payne. It was a blur as it flew at Shayne. His left hand shot up, the glove snapped closed and the net rippled from where the puck hit.

"Will they pull him? Mom? Are they going to pull him?"

She watched the replay, her hand over her mouth as

they commentators told of a time out called. God. No. Oh no.

"Mom?" Carmen grabbed her arm, as nervous as Lacey felt. She couldn't remember the last time Shayne had been pulled. It happened. But so early in the season? "Mom," her youngest whispered as the camera followed Shayne off the ice then his replacement on.

"Shayne," Lacey whispered. She saw the way his glove smacked against the Plexiglas. "Phone. Phone!"

Carmen scrambled around looking for her and handed it to her. Lacey's hand was shaking as she stared at the number pad for several seconds.

"One," Carmen whispered and reached over and pressed one. "Eight. Three. Two."

Lacey pushed aside Carmen's hand and finished the remaining numbers on her own. "Turn it off."

Kayla aimed the remote at the TV and the screen went black.

Lacey stood up and walked down the hall.

"You saw."

She covered her mouth, nodding as she leaned against the wall. He sounded so tired. She slid down, not really aware of Kayla walking by as she went into Lacey's room. "Baby," she said softly because it's all that could come out of her tight throat.

"I'm shit, Lace. I couldn't find the puck with a binocular. It's all shit." He sighed heavily and she rested her elbow on her knees as tears slipped down. "Two games, Lace. Two." She heard a loud bang and knew something had been kicked. Or thrown. "I've won two fucking games. It's like there are holes in my glove. Fuck!"

He yelled and she gripped the phone. "I gotta go, Lace. I'm...I'm...I'll call later."

"Shayne." But he hung up, leaving her with silence. He was hurting so much. He was so far away. She hadn't talked to him since he left. He hadn't called either. Tonight though she couldn't not call.

She should've called sooner. She rubbed her thumb over the hearing end of the phone. He would've been just as hurting in the pre-season. It was that glove smack that had done it for her. And Carmen.

Lowering the phone, Lacey stared at the opposite wall. She had to go to him. She had to go because he was hurting. Nodding to herself, she stood up and walked into her room.

Kayla and Carmen were haphazardly shoving clothing into her suitcase so it looked like Carmen's bulging backpack months ago. She began to take items out.

"Mom! You have to go!"

Lacey began to refold her clothes, laying them smoothly in the suitcase. "I know." She looked at her eldest daughter. "This is why you came home, isn't it?"

"We were going to push you on the plane. You're crying, Mom, all the time. Carm called me. She didn't know what to do. When she told me about Shayne, I knew." Kayla shrugged a shoulder. "Now you do too."

Lacey looked at her youngest daughter. Poor Carmen. It was easy to forget that underneath it all she was still a fifteen year old kid. Dealing with her mother's heartache was unfair. "Hey." She reached over and batted her youngest on the arm. "I'm the grown up here, not you. Remember that."

Carmen nodded as she handed her a refolded top. "Mom. After you fix Shayne, you have to fix Uncle Todd. Something's going on with him."

Lacey nodded. These men of hers were a mess. "So," she looked at Kayla who was the organizer out of her girls, "I'm assuming you have a plan."

Her daughter knew how to plan. Kayla had already booked a flight for Lacey. Now she stood in front of a large silver and glass building that did not look like Shayne at all. Her stomach was jittery. During the drive into Regina, she hadn't been nervous. Through her six-hour flight, she hadn't been nervous.

Now, she was nervous.

She dug out the phone she had bought at the airport. Expensive little bugger but she had stopped at the kiosk and impulsively bought it. Cash and trash, the guy had described the prepaid phone as. She stood in front of the unfamiliar building and dialled the familiar number.

"Donnelly."

Her hand tightened on the handle of her suitcase. "Hi," she said softly.

"Lacey."

Just that. It was enough. Tears filled her eyes and she wiped them away. She reached over and opened the door to the building and dragged her suitcase in.

"It says blocked. Why are you blocked?"

She lied. Bad her. "Funny thing. Came home, found Kayla on my couch." Not a lie. "It's her phone as Carmen's hogging the other one." There was the lie. She stared at the panel before her. His name wasn't listed but Todd had told her his condo number to enter. "I wanted to hear your voice."

She entered the right number and listened to the speaker buzz.

"Hang on."

She nodded as she lowered the phone. His voice was tinny through the speaker. "I have a delivery--it needs a signature."

"Get the guy downstairs to sign."

She looked at the security guard. "No one there."

"Right. Come on up."

Lacey grabbed the door as he released the lock then she walked in, dragging her suitcase behind her. The guy looked up then down when she gave a little wave.

"Sorry," Shayne said as he returned to the phone. "It's just...fuck, Lace."

"I know." She hit the elevator button and wished she were already upstairs with him. Her nerves were gone. He was so hurting. Would she lose the call? How she hated these stupid phones.

She stepped into the elevator and hit twelve. "Do you know what I realized when I saw Kayla last night? She's growing up. That city's no good for her. Turning her into an adult on me. When did she get to be almost twenty, Shayne?"

"Beats me. I'm still processing Carmen is fifteen and not five."

"You're keeping yourself too open," she said as she watched the numbers climb. "Coach would tell you to not stand like a starfish." His bark of laughter made her heart hurt. She tightened her hand on the suitcase grip then stepped off and tried to figure where the hell his place was. She went left, turned around and went the other way. At the door she paused and ran her hand over the wood. "Then he'd tell you you're not a rookie and to smarten the fuck up."

She knocked.

"Yeah. He would. Hang on. Someone's at the door. Delivery."

"Okay." She stared down the hallway and really couldn't imagine him living here. The door opened and she turned to stare into his hurting hazel eyes. "So, guess what my daughters did?"

"Lace."

She closed the phone, shoving it into her pocket and flung herself at him. Those familiar arms wrapped around her and he lifted her up to bury his face in her neck. He felt the same. Thank God, he felt the same. There was a little clatter as he tossed his phone aside then fisted his hand on the back of her shirt. He was shaking. Her big ice warrior was shaking. She smoothed her hand over the back of his neck.

"I really wanted you here," he whispered by her ear, his voice raspy. "It's all going to shit, Lacey. It's all...and when you called last night, all I wanted was you."

"You've got me. Sorry it took so long to get here." She kissed the base of his neck and tightened her arms around him. She wasn't entirely sure she'd ever be able to let go again. Not that she was planning on it. He was hers. She was keeping him. No more can'ts. "Customs was a bitch."

Bio

Jenna's writing dreams truly began one summer on the air mattress of her childhood home. There she tackled her first romance: a truly wretched attempt at a medieval historical. Upon finishing the purple prose laden story of (in her own words) crap, Jenna decided that perhaps the historical genre wasn't for her and she promptly began to write in a contemporary setting. If only the journey had been easy. She tackled category romances (and in her own words) felt like they were crap. She didn't have the patience for romantic suspense. Really, she just wanted to get to writing the sex. (hint hint, Jenna) Her romantic comedies were so traumatic that she stopped writing until one day she got a phone call from a friend who said "We can totally write this." The genre was erotic romance and it was (in her own words) like coming home. Residing in Calgary, Alberta, Jenna happily writes the naughty romances that make her mother sooooo comfortable. (not)

www.jennahoward.com